AS WE WENT TO BED

A mother, a lover and something else

KRITIKA SHARMA

BOOKS BY KRITIKA SHARMA

FICTION:

As We Went To Bed

The Rogue Spy – The Delhi Chapter (Book 1)

Desires Series
Treacherous Desires (Book 1)
Desires Revisited (Book 2)

Ghost Series
Live-in with a Ghost (Book 1)
In Love with a Ghost (Book 2)
Forever with a Ghost (Book 3)

Jab We Quarantined (Short Read)
Be My Quarantine (Short Read)

The Slut Chronicles Series:
Betrayed (Book 1)
Enslaved (Book 2)
Obsessed (Book 3)

Perfect Crimes Series:
The Girl Who Died: Perfect Crimes Episode 1
The Stolen Diamonds: Perfect Crimes Episode 2
The Silent Death: Perfect Crimes Episode 3

NON-FICTION:
Manage your Manager

AS WE WENT TO BED

A mother, a lover and something else

KRITIKA SHARMA

KALAMOS LITERARY SERVICES LLP

Kalamos Literary Services LLP
Email: info@kalamos.co.in | editorial@kalamos.co.in

First Published in 2024
by
Kalamos Literary Services

ISBN- 978-81-19601-72-1

As We Went To Bed
Kritika Sharma

Cover designed & typeset in Kalamos Literary Services LLP
Edited by Priyanka Lal & Brand Inspire
(info@brandinspire.in)
Print and bound in India.

Dedicated to all the girls
who suffer in one form or another.

Although this is a work of fiction, the issues portrayed are undeniably real in the lives of many.

PROLOGUE
THE START OF A CHANGE

The alarm blared off and I sat up straight. It was the crack of dawn, and I rubbed my eyes to check the time. The darkness still swelling from the windows, I peered at the clock. Five in the morning… it came too soon, I thought groggily as I walked out of the bed and dragged myself to the bathroom.

The small light in the bathroom flooded the room, putting my family in focus. My husband, my son and daughter are sleeping peacefully, without any care in the world. Good! My kids deserve that, so does my husband. I sighed as I walked in the bathroom to start another damn day!

So, who am I? I am Nyra Manchanda, mother of two incredibly beautiful children and the usual corporate sucker who lives and dies for the whims of the managers they serve.

I am almost thirty-five now, and it feels like I have already spent more than half of my life under the thumb of the miserable corporate rule. But well, what am I complaining about, I have chosen this life.

But maybe today it will change, I thought as I kicked out the yoga mat after freshening up and tried to focus on my breathing. Today I have an interview for a new job, for the position of Director in Polar Technologies, and if I get it, maybe I would get out of this rut of life and be in another one!

I was still mulling over, if I should even take this interview when a sudden burst of cries filled the house. Damn! I did not even get five minutes of deep breathing. I stood up and walked to the kitchen to prepare a bottle of milk for my daughter, Ojaswi, aka Ojha. She is only four years old, while my son is seven.

After making sure Ojha is asleep again, I hurry back to the kitchen and prepare a glass of milk for my son, Shivaya, aka Shiv, he needs to wake up in another fifteen minutes or he would be late for the school–again!

And so goes my life…

"Best of luck," my husband, Dhruv, wished me as he flopped on the sofa set and stared at his laptop intently. He too is a corporate man but in a different organization. Like me, he too is in a senior position but he, unlike me, commands a certain respect in his company, which I am grateful for. But hey, it does not matter what position you are in, it is a piss-off life everywhere.

I muttered him a thanks as I made sure Ojha was playing safely in the vicinity of his vision, and closed the door shut. Shiv is at school, he is in 2nd standard now. Ojha is in KG but as she was running a fever this morning, I decided not to send her today.

"You will keep on eye on her?" I popped my head out of the room and asked Dhruv.

He shot me a look filled with such incredulity that I couldn't help but laugh. He playfully jerked his head, indicating how absurd it was for me to even ask that. But hey, a mother is always worried, and the last thing I need today is for my daughter to fall on her head, requiring me to rush out of the interview.

And so there went my first interview. And the guy who took it was an ass, to be honest. He asked me absurd questions and I knew deep down he would be a blocker for me to move ahead. Yet I answered all the questions, keeping a deep smile pasted on my lips and spent good forty-five minutes with him. By the end of the interview, I felt I had impressed him, but his smirk said otherwise. "The HR will get back to you, Nyra," he smiled at me. "But you seem way too overqualified for what we need a candidate for!"

"Okay…." I trailed off.

"But the HR will get back to you," he smiled, waved at the camera for my benefit and then disconnected after some formal, usual greetings.

"Asshole!" I cursed as I slammed the laptop shut.

I knew right then, I have not cracked this interview.

And I just went on with my day and life, churning the corporate wheels, rubbing in the grease, spending endless days and nights working and taking care of two adorable, adorable children.

But I was surprised when after twenty odd days I got another call from the same company, Polar Technologies, I had interviewed for.

"Hey, Nyra," the man spoke.

I had saved his number the last time, so I was shocked to hear his questioning tone.

"Hey Rohan, how are you?" I asked. Hated, I him, but I could not help putting on my chirpy self. Well, to be honest, Rohan did not do anything to me, that asshole on the interview did. But well, person from the same company, so potayto-potahto!

"I am doing good. Just calling to check if you heard anything from Avinash?" Rohan asked.

Avinash, the asshole who took the first interview, had said that the HR will get back, and I relayed the same to Rohan.

"Oh, I did not hear anything from him, and he has gone on a vacation. I am incredibly sorry to ask you but would you mind re-doing the interview with another lead?" Rohan spoke. And maybe the universe was finally looking out for me.

"Okay," I paused for dramatic effect, and then added, "When?"

"Today? Sorry this is so sudden, but we have an urgent requirement, and you have an excellent profile. So our department head wants to interview you himself!" Rohan chirped.

"Alright," I replied, and we quickly set up the time. It was not easy with my schedule and also the man's who was the supposed head of the department. We had to fix it for 10PM that night, but it was alright for me. I, anyway, always worked late nights post putting my kids to bed.

After sharing the turn of events to Dhruv on the call, who was in his office, I continued with my work.

As usual, I worked my ass off, braced the heat from a rather difficult client, cooked dinner for my kids, cajoled or should I say forced them to eat it without a lot of screen time, and then put them to bed.

All in all, I was done by 9:30PM and my nerves were wracking. I really needed a new job because the current one was killing me. And no, I had no nannies because I had a very sour–incredibly sour experience when Shiv was one year old with one of them and I was done with the whole concept of nannies altogether!

Ten o' clock came and so did the call. I plastered an incredible smile on my face, Rohan introduced me to the head and dropped off. Shlok Rajput… and he was good. Not an asshole at all, and by the sounds of it, and the way he interviewed me, I think he liked me. Although it was ten in the night when we started and ended at 11:30PM, it did not seem like this man was tired at all. But well, I was. I was yawning by the end of it, and it was my non-stop yawns post 11:15PM that made him laugh and forced him to disconnect the call.

"I am sorry," he had smiled, "your stories are so fascinating, I have been looking for someone with your experience and expertise," he had chimed at the end. "But sleep well now, Nyra, while I am sure I am going to take you, I would like you to talk to one of your future peers to understand what would be expected out of you. If you agree with the work, well, I will then start seeing you in our offices."

I had beamed with pride at these words. My current manager did not appreciate my experience or expertise, but in just one call, Shlok did. And while I still had one last hurdle to cross, I knew I was going to take this job, whatever maybe the scenario!

Around midnight, as I narrated highlights of my interview to Dhruv, who I knew was not listening to me, since he was staring at his phone in rapt attention, I realised how happy I was.

And as we went to bed that night, with a smile plastered on my face, one that had been missing for years on end, I knew, I would remember this day forever. Because today was the day, when my so-called perfect life started to go downhill; when it all had started to change.

1 HAPPINESS IS ALSO RELATIVE!

It took me three months and eight days to start with the position in Shlok's team in Polar Technologies. And by the time it happened, Shiv was in 3rd standard and Ojha was in 1st. Kids grow up so fast, parents just cannot tell.

So yeah, it took me three months because my ex-manager did not let me go. Can you believe I worked for that man for two years and that man did not bother to talk to me even ten times in that span? And whenever I needed his support, he just dismissed me saying I was too senior for my own good and should be dealing with my problems on my own!

Well, when I resigned from that godawful position, he had asked what he could do to make me stay! And I had hit him back with his very words that apparently, my manager was my problem, and well, I have dealt with my problem on my own by finding a much better one.

In that moment I had felt he had cursed me, and while I did not believe in things like curses, but the way shit unfurled on me in the coming months, I now do believe that yes, curses do exist and can come true.

So, I started work with Shlok and as I had expected, it was a whirlwind of sorts. I was used to working late hours, but this was something else. It was tremendous pressure and super strenuous, and by the end of the first month, I felt drained out. But hey, I chose it, so no complaining. But if I were twenty-five-year-old at this time, I would have embraced it fully because then I had nothing else to do, but now, I have two small children to take care of, and I just cannot let my career upend their lives. But there was no having it.

Shlok was the best manager I have had in my life. I have fifteen years of experience (yes, I started work when I was twenty, now I think about it, yes, I was too young and stupid to do it,) but that is a story for another day! Back to Shlok—yes, best manager ever. Way too intelligent, way too smart, and way too charming for his own benefit. Barely thirty-eight years old, still single, an incredible flirt and playboy—or so I have heard from a few people I have interacted with in my first month—and the youngest president in the organisation. What he did in his personal life was not my care but on professional front, I could only think of him as a beast, or a machine perhaps because he worked more than twenty hours a day and never slept. I honestly did not understand how he even functioned. But well, who cares. He knew about my family situation and till the time he respected that, I was fine with whatever this job demanded of me.

But it did not happen! I became so busy and constantly tired that my kids started to lag in their studies and daily school work. Yes, they are barely in 1st and 3rd class as of now, but it is a ruthless world. And I, for one, hated myself on seeing Shiv getting 44 out of 50 in his midterm exams. I know 44 is good, but he had never gotten anything less than 48 ever in the past, like ever… well, hello, genius mom here who was once some kind of child prodigy, but this 44 did it.

And while I did not show my disappointment to him, I knew Shiv was far more upset than I was. And hence, I enrolled my kids for tuitions, for the first time. And not just tuitions, in day care too. So yeah, now my kids stayed at school till 2PM, then they left for tuition-cum-day care around 4PM and came back at around 8PM. Yep, shitty life, but what can we say, life is not fair.

And while I got a serious backlash from my in-laws for putting the kids in day care for so damn long, and not taking care of them like a good mother, I knew it was best for all of us. For starters, my kids loved that day care because they now had good ten other children to play with for four long hours, and they were incredibly happy. And so was I… so damn much. Because another guilt that always ate me from within was that I was not able to let my kids play in the park or gardens like other kids because, sigh! I just did not have the time. I had tried taking them to the park, to play with other kids, on play dates, but my hectic work schedule always never allowed me to. And it was upsetting. But this day care helped, and I wondered why I did not opt for it before.

And as I closed the panel of my laptop on my first month work anniversary, also the first day when kids spent a very happy day in the day care, I shared with Dhruv how I was finally feeling settled now. But he was not listening, as usual. He was on his phone again, staring at his screen. But I did not care. Our kids were sleeping blissfully between us—we have a massive *triple* bed in our room, where Dhruv and I slept on opposite ends, Shiv and Ojha slept in the middle—and the sight of them content and too damn tired with all the play made me happy. I smiled as I turned off the lights, and while still smiling to myself, as we went to bed that night, I thought, finally, I was happy. But considering, in my case happiness is also relative, I was as happy as I could be in the house I always called my 'home sweet home'.

2
OH! BEAUTIFUL, AM I?

I have spent more than a month working with Shlok, and unfortunately, so far, I have only worked with Shlok in the company.

He had a wide team, and while he held fortnightly calls with his full team for updates and announcements, I have actually not talked to anyone for a longer span! I have talked to people here and there, tried to understand the nuances of the company and ways of working here but that was the extent of it. I only interacted with Shlok and it was not because of anything secretive on his part, it was mainly because I was working on a super important proposal for a client that the Polar Technologies had been trying to sign for months now, and it was still very doubtful.

And, it was for this client, I was now asked to travel to Bangalore.

"I am not going alone," I announced on the call to Shlok.

"I think you can handle it," Shlok assured me.

"Umm… no, not at all, I am still learning the ways here. No way I am going down there alone. If you have to throw someone to the wolves, throw someone else, but I am not it!"

"I do not have anyone to send with you," Shlok sighed. It was an audio call, I could hear how defeated he sounded.

"And honestly, until this deal is signed, I do not have budget for two people too," he added glumly.

"I do not care, Shlok, if you have budget for one person, then go yourself because I do not want Mihira to say that I fucked up this meeting," I blasted. He had been hinting for a week that I may have to go down to Bangalore and meet the CFO—fucking Chief Financial Officer—of a billion-dollar conglomerate–alone! A CFO, who was a good friend of Mihira, our CMO—Chief Marketing Officer. I mean, come on!

He did not react to my pronouncement, and I realised I had said too much.

"I am sorry," I spoke softly.

"For what?" he demanded. "For suggesting that I am throwing you to wolves or for your choice of words?"

"Latter," I sighed. "I often forget to reign my tongue when I am agitated."

"I have seen that," he was gruff. "And while I do not mind your tongue as much, you suggesting that I would throw you to wolves, hurts. As if I do not care for you…"

"Then act like it; come with me," I suggested.

"But—" he started but I interjected. "You proposed that I go there, attend the meeting, stay the night, and return the next day. But why don't we both go down there, and come back the same day?"

"Have you ever been to Bangalore, Nyra?" he demanded, and I could tell he was supressing his laughter.

"I have been to many places, but I have never had the displeasure of getting stuck in the traffic of Bangalore, Shlok," I laughed now. "But I have checked the client offices, they are actually not in the main city but quite close to the airport. So, a day trip is perfectly feasible."

And while he did not react to the details, I had taken the initiative to plan this trip, and I could sense he was impressed, or at the very least, he agreed to join me…..

We flew a week later.

I had to make a few arrangements with Dhruv to ensure that the kids were dropped off and picked up on time. And while I knew Dhruv was an incredibly responsible and loving father, I had to ensure he did not miss it. Afterall, it was I who always took care of the kids. He supports, yes. Actually, he supports much more than any other man I know, but still, being a mother, the primary responsibility of the kids always falls on me, naturally!

Shlok and I took an early flight on Thursday morning. Our meeting with the CFO was at noon, so we took the flight at 6AM, which meant I was at the airport at 4AM, which meant I left home at 2:30AM, while I worked till two on the presentation we were supposed to deliver that day.

I was exhausted. But as they say, no rest for the wicked, I was still working on the presentation frantically as I waited for boarding when I noticed two legs standing quite close to my seat.

And there he was… grinning broadly at me, his eyes a bit too sleep deprived, standing a mere foot away.

"Good morning," he said with a smile.

It was the first time I was seeing him in person, and I really did not like the soft sensation that swirled in my body, but it was small, just very small and quite easy to push down. Thanks to the work-from-home policy from Covid days, I had not set foot in office premises so far. And honestly, I had not seen his face since that first interview I had with him—Shlok never turned on his camera on official calls, I had often wondered why!

"Good morning," I replied with a smile too and he slumped on the seat beside me.

"You are early here," he commented.

"Umm, you are actually late," I chuckled as I pointed at the line that was now boarding our flight and was almost done.

"Why did you not board?" he asked as I packed my laptop.

"I was waiting for you. No way I was going to get on that plane without my big boss," I laughed.

And he laughed with me. His laughter was so breezy, so light, that I could not help but feel a light flutter down my spine.

"Big boss, hey?" he chuckled.

"That's you, aren't you?" I beamed as we headed to board the flight.

"What are you going to do on the flight?" he yawned, and I knew why. He had been working with me on the presentation till two this morning. "I think I am going to pass out," he added.

"I cannot sleep on a plane, so I am going to stare at the clouds and see the beautiful morning," I smiled.

"You are a star gazer, are you?" he asked with mild curiosity.

"Nature is beautiful, and I like to appreciate it," I commented as I handed my boarding pass at the gate to step through.

"Well, I appreciate all kinds of beauty," he commented in such sincere tone that I felt a jolt in my stomach. I looked up at him and I swear I saw him avert his eyes from my face right that moment.

And though I did not get into bed that night, as I buckled my seat belt, four rows away from where Shlok sat in the plane, I closed my eyes and wondered what he meant.

While he was beautiful, oh yes he was, with his charming smile, the twinkle in his eyes, his chiselled jaw, his light beard and unruly hair that stuck out at the back, I was nothing in comparison. I was a girl who once was very popular and beautiful but has now gone to seed. I now was overweight—

a result of major illness and two pregnancies and a certain mental disorder—and had marks of various allergies all over my once pretty face, and the confidence had gone to drain with every kilo I had put on in the past years. So, yeah, I was too damn sure he did not mean I was beautiful when he gave me that fleeting look. Because who would find me beautiful when my own husband does not… who would want me when my own husband… well… story for another day!

3 YEP! MY DOWNFALL

"That's why I did not want to come," Shlok stretched his arms once the meeting was over. It lasted five hours and I was totally drained. Shlok had slept throughout the 2.5 hours plane journey, but damn my mind, it just cannot sleep while moving. So, now I was feeling seriously sleep deprived, thanks to pulling two full all-nighters for this meeting.

"I think it went well; I am quite sure we will get the project," I chimed in, stifling a yawn.

"When did you last sleep?" Misha intervened. Misha was also part of Polar Technologies and was based in Bangalore. Shlok wanted her to be the face of the project so that she could build in-person relationships with the client while I managed from Delhi office. This pissed me off rather brutally when Shlok had introduced me to Misha in the morning. Why should some other girl build relationships with my client when I was doing all the heavy lifting, but well, the alternative was for me to shift to Bangalore, which was never an option! Dhruv hated Bangalore's traffic and kids were well settled in Delhi, and in no scenario, I would uproot their life and move them for a damn project!

"I think I slept on Monday last," I spoke as I stifled another yawn.

"Shame on you, Shlok," Misha reprimanded, "she has not slept for three nights now, no wonder she looks dead on her feet. Why would you do that to her?"

Shlok did give me a very concerned look, but I just shook my head.

"Take the day off tomorrow and rest," Shlok suggested. "If anything will come, I will handle it."

"I was anyway going to do that, you know," and this time I just could not stifle a rather wide yawn.

"That's good then," and there it was again, his charming smile that took the breath of many girls, I believe Misha's for sure because she was staring at him like he was a sweet candy she could not wait to taste.

I had not realised when the flights were booked that while our flight to Bangalore was same, our return flight was different. They were fifteen minutes apart—he chose Indigo and I chose Air India; I have my reasons for choosing Air India over Indigo. As I started for the airport, alone, Shlok decided to spend some more time with Misha, I felt upset. If only I had forethought of asking him which was his flight! But why do I even care…?

I shook my head like a wet dog and called Dhruv to check up on the kids. It was almost time to pick them up from the day care. And as it happens, Dhruv, the best father of the year, was already on his way to pick them up. He had also decided what he would order for the kids for dinner and had promised me to put them to sleep before I came back home—which I knew would be after midnight.

As predicted, the trip from the client offices to airport was quick and I arrived almost an hour early. So, I parked myself on a seat near the boarding gate and fired up my laptop. But this time I did not work. I was too exhausted to work. So instead, I opened up a word file and started writing.

I have a secret that only a handful people in my family know. I am a writer and I write the mushiest, the most swoon worthy romance novels. But I write them under a pen name. Not because I write dirty stuff, well, 'dirty' was not something I dabbled in any form, but because in my romance stories I pour my heart out, my desires out, and that was something I do not want people to read with my name on.

Keeping an eye on the clock, I started writing a new romantic story, and it chimed away. The first announcement to board the flight was made, and a few minutes later Shlok's flight was announced too. Apparently and coincidentally, our boarding gates were right next to each other.

Then the second announcement was made.

He must be coming… I thought.

Then the third announcement.

Where the hell was he?

Final announcement.

I know I should move… I know I should go, but somehow, I could not lift my feet from the floor. Somehow, I could not go until I had said goodbye to the man who meant nothing to me. I wonder why that was.

"This is the final announcement for the boarding of Flight–" and I knew it was my cue because it was my gate, my flight, and all the passengers had already gone inside.

I heaved a sigh as the face of my kids flashed in front of my eyes and I packed up my laptop. I almost stood up and there he was, running towards me, to board the flight. He ran past me, stopped abruptly, shook hands, wished me a good flight, and ran inside.

So did I….

As I sat in the plane, smiling to myself only God knows why, a message popped on my WhatsApp.

Thanks for all the work, it was a good day. It was a message from Shlok and a wide grin spread on my face as I read it. He was appreciating my work; that's what I had always wanted in my career.

Thanks for supporting me throughout and coming down here with me, I answered.

Of course, he replied.

I waited, wondering what I should say next. Or even if I should say anything when another text popped up.

What were you doing till now? Working?

I chuckled at the message, though there was nothing to laugh there.

I was not working, I replied simply.

I saw you, it was not a 'not working' look, he answered.

Seriously, not working, I replied but I could not help the grin on my face.

Then what? he insisted.

And I did not know why, but I wanted to tell him; so I did.

Actually, I am also a writer, and I was working on my next book.

Silence on the other end.

Next book? he was sceptical.

I have published six books so far, I informed.

And he sent a 'jaw dropping' emoji.

I laughed out loud this time.

Send me the link, he wrote eagerly.

I cannot, I write under a pen name, I sighed.

Why? he demanded.

For reasons unknown to you, and I grinned again.

Hmm… send me the link anyway. I promise I won't judge, he replied.

And there was something in the last five words of his message that I pulled the link of my latest book and sent to him.

Silence for a long moment.

The plane was moving now, and I knew I would have to turn off the phone now. Maybe he was already in the air and had already done it. But then he replied, *National Bestselling Author, wow! Amazing!*

Thanks… do you read books? I asked, unsure whether I want him to read my work or not. Thriller was fine, but this pure romance for my manager to read, geez!

Yes. I don't read romance though, he replied with a smile.

It is fine, no one I know reads, so…

Hmm… was all he replied.

Good night, Shlok.

Good night, try to sleep some, he replied instantly.

I seriously cannot sleep. I am just gonna stare at the black horizon.

Haha! he replied.

Pause.

Then replied again, *But seriously, Nyra, it is just so amazing that you write. Unbelievable.*

And as the lights dimmed in the plane, I realized we had already taken off and were mid-air, and the network had disappeared from my phone.

And as I went to bed that night, I knew I was in deep shit. Because the smile that had appeared on my face since I had started chatting with him on WhatsApp was still etched on my face. And somehow, deep down I knew, this boy, this charming, gorgeous boy, would be my downfall. Yep! My downfall and the downfall of all the walls I have built around me.

4 FAN-FUCKING-TASTIC!

I slept through the Friday, duh! But as expected, it ruined my weekend.

Not because I was unable to sleep or function but because owing to all the sleep I got on Friday afternoon, I found none at night. And I decided to talk to Dhruv, a mistake, a big mistake.

"Won't you even ask how my trip was or how did the meeting go?" I asked Dhruv once I knew both the kids were asleep.

"Huh! I asked you," Dhruv smiled.

"When?" I wondered in shock. "Did you perhaps ask when I was deep asleep?"

And a groggy look came over his face. He was tired, I know. As I had been sleeping throughout the day, waking up only to make meals for everyone and then sleeping again, it meant that it was Dhruv who had to do the heavy lifting for second day in a row. He sent the kids, brought them back, fed them, changed them—well, overall, took care of them in short.

"Maybe, sorry" he mumbled. And I knew he was short moments away from snoring.

And there it goes! Snore, snore, snore. I just had to pause for two long minutes, and he was snoring like a hippo!

Tears trickled down my face as I saw his sleeping form and wondered what went wrong between us.

I met Dhruv when I was twenty years old. He and I were once in the same organization, him being two years senior. We fell in love, or was it really love? I do not know what love truly was, but I liked him really. And our meeting and first conversation is another story altogether.

I was very young, as anyone can imagine, when I joined the first company I ever worked for. Barely twenty, I was fresh out of college and was ready to take on the world. And I should take pride, but I was… no, well, I *am* very intelligent and sharp-minded person. Within months of joining of my first company, I was leading a project, Dhruv being the overall client lead. And before I had turned 21, I was promoted—the fastest promotion ever, or so I was told. And I was quite nice looking too back then; I was told by at least a dozen guys in the company who sought out some or the other relationship with me back then. One even went as far as to introduce me to his mother when, *ahem*, I was not even his girlfriend but was just a casual friend! Anyway, whatever the others may be up to, I had eyes only for one man. Dhruv Singh Manchanda was a charming manager. He was good looking, very kind natured and a patient man—a quality I always sought. He was also ambitious, the good kind. And that was my nucleus. A nice, kind natured, soft-spoken man who was ambitious, well, bring it on! And before I turned 22, I was married to him.

But as it turned out, his charming and attractive personality was the extent of it all.

While Dhruv was incredibly loving and charming man, he was just my friend… yep, only a friend! I realised it on our wedding night when I felt no chemistry when he touched me. And I knew he felt the same because, well, he did not touch me a lot post that. I craved for his touch, his love, his attention, but damn, was that man not interested. But he was my best friend, the best-est friend I could ever dream of, and I did not mind the other thing.

I still wonder why I did not mind that too much, maybe because of how I grew up, or maybe because of the family I grew up in that I felt….

Well, I do not know what I felt back then, but today, fourteen fucking years in a platonic marriage and silence, I feel it was a shitty deal, and absolute stupidity on my part to ignore that big facet of my life that was the crux of all sorts of satisfaction!

The next morning, Saturday, I had woken up very solemn, but he did not have a care in the world. He just went about his day, played some video games, spent time with the kids, while I… I just stewed in my misery, curled up in front of the Netflix and binged watch the entire first season with eight episodes of a new series. I was in the kitchen, making dinner for the kids, when he found me.

"What you doing?" he asked casually. "Any way I can help?"

I just shook my head and continued making the *parathas* that I always cooked for the kids.

He closed the kitchen door and asked seriously, "What's wrong?"

"What could be wrong?" I shrugged carelessly.

"Okay, how was the meeting?" he asked finally. And despite myself, tears spilled down my face.

"I was too tired yesterday, Nyra, don't cry."

"Why would I cry when it took you forty hours to ask me how my day was; despite me complaining that you did not ask! You could have asked me at any moment during the day, but you did not!" I sniffled.

"Okay, I am asking now, how was it?" he smiled casually. "And did you get it?"

I exhaled loudly, "We may get it, yes," I nodded.

"That's great! And oh, I forgot to tell you," he hesitated, "mom, dad have to attend a wedding in Delhi, so they will be visiting us for a week."

My jaw dropped at the announcement.

"A week?" I stammered.

"Yes, they thought, since they are coming all the way here so maybe they can spend some time with the kids," he smiled.

And I exhaled the breath I was not even aware of holding. "Of course, they are your parents, they should come and visit," I smiled.

"Kids would be so happy, it is a surprise, so don't tell them," and he grinned broadly.

And I nodded.

Yes, they were his parents; parents who absolutely loved and adored their only son and two grandchildren. But they were *his* parents, not mine. And no matter what they showcased on social media, yep, my father-in-law was very active on social media and called me his *DIL*, not just a daughter-in-law, but his heart as he always tried to portray, but I was nothing of that sort. I was the black sheep of the family who was a rebel and did not listen to a damn thing. And they were coming here.

Fan-fucking-tastic! I swore under my breath the moment Dhruv left the kitchen to attend to the kids, who were now fighting.

As my life was going to get difficult, I dropped a WhatsApp to Shlok saying I would be working on and off in the coming week.

All okay? he asked instantly.

Long story, but while I will work, I may not be as available, and my apologies in advance.

What's wrong? he added, and my heart melted at his concern.

Tell you sometime later? I asked.

Sure… take your time. I will see you when I see you.

I wanted to ask when he would see me again. I wanted to see him again, but did not dwell on that thought much. I, maybe, will ask him later when he planned to visit the office, but tonight was not the night.

And as we went to bed that night, I dreaded the coming week which was bound to be fan-fucking-tastic. And while Dhruv's snores filled up the room and the kids slept peacefully between us, my thoughts staggered to a stop at the face of one man who was not my husband, but always gave rise to flutters in my heart every time I even thought of him. As I blinked in the darkness, his smiling face flashed in front of my eyes, and it made me wonder many things. What was he to me, I did not know, but I knew I was just a mere employee to him and no matter what happened in the future, I would make sure that would not change. He would always stay my big boss, and I, well, I would be one of the twenty other team members he has.

5 BUT WAS ENOUGH EVER ENOUGH?

I woke up with a start.... It was Sunday, so I had slept in like usual, which generally helps me recharge and be fresh, but I felt clammy. I was drenched in sweat. What happened to me? I wondered as I looked at the clock in our room, it was just after ten in the morning. No, the question should be, what happened to him!

I gulped down a lot of water as I tried to remember the nightmare I just had. And it was so vivid and clear. I had dreamed that I was roaming around in a street, not of Delhi, but ironically of Jaipur, where I had grown up. Alas, all my nightmares were always of that city, of the old house where I had grown up or of the school where I was tortured for twelve ruddy years! So the dream.... I was on my old bicycle when I got his call. I picked it up with a smile... he told me he is in a gym. As if my soul soared, flying out of my body, I saw him lifting heavy weights in a dimly lit gym. My soul-form watched my body laughing at what he had just said but could not hear the conversation.

Suddenly, he gets hurt, brutally hurt, and calls for help. And now, my bodily self is panicking, my soul-self is panicking because he is hurt, and I do not know what to do. I race around on my stupid white bicycle, but I do not even know where he lives... I am panting, I am struggling, I am crying to help him, he needs me, he needs me… and then I had woken up!

I rubbed my eyes as I realised it was the first dream I ever had of Shlok, and it felt like a warning to me. Stupid me… but I had to know. So, I picked up my phone and sent him a quick WhatsApp text–

Are you okay? I wrote, then feeling it would be too childish and borderline crazy to send, especially to my boss, I deleted it and wrote instead, *Any message from the client yesterday?*

And then pausing, I added, *So that I am prepared for tomorrow!*

He did not reply instantly; his last seen was two hours ago….

I waited patiently in bed, not yet willing to step out of the room because I knew once I was out of the room, I would not have a moment's peace until I crawled back into the bed at night, absolutely drained.

His message came, and it read, *No news is good news.*

And I exhaled in relief. Of course, it was just a stupid nightmare. I saw him in my dreams because I was thinking about him when I had dozed off. There was nothing to it; I should not read much into it… and I paused at my own thought and stressed to myself, 'I definitely do not need to read too much into it.' And then swearing to myself that I would restart listening to audiobooks before going to sleep to keep my nightmares revolving around the story of the book, I stepped out of the bed, out of my room, to plant a good morning kiss on my children's head and start the day.

Dhruv and I spent the entire day cleaning the house. My in-laws were due to arrive on Monday morning from Lucknow, and I was beyond ecstatic… oh sorry, I meant, frantic. But what can I do! When I had gotten married to Dhruv all those years ago, I was very happy. I was the happiest person on the planet back then. Well, I am kind of still happy with him, if you remove a few parameters from the equation, but it is all fine. However, when I got married, no one had told me that you do not just get married to the boy, you get married to the whole plethora of family that's attached to him.

The same could be said for the husband too, but hey, at least in India, husbands are not forced to live or abide by the rules dictated by the girls' parents, isn't it? The guy is always treated as a king by any girl's parents, and the girl, well, let's just say, it is too long a story to discuss.

Anyway, coming back to the frantic situation at hand, we cleaned—from fans to the floor, from shelves of the bathroom to the kitchen. No, my house was not that filthy, I do have a maid who helps me with cleaning and dusting, but come on, I am a working mother, and I have limitations. I just cannot monitor every minute what my maid cleans, or notice the minute specks of dirt even, for that matter. But my in-laws....

So, yes, we cleaned. Together, like a family. And by the time we went to bed on Sunday night, I could help but feel the hatred for my in-laws boil in my veins. Every torment they have made me endure in the past years, every comment they have passed, everything they have done to make me suffer, to turn me into a submissive housewife, reverberated in my head. And despite myself, despite deciding years ago to be quiet and calm in their presence as they only came for a few days to harass me, I promised myself, if they gave me troubles this time, and if Dhruv did not stand up for me this time, I will take charge and I will stand up for myself. Because after fourteen damn years, enough was enough.

THEY CAME, THEY FOUGHT, AND I LOST 6

My in-laws arrived at ten in the morning… I was preparing tea for them in the kitchen while Dhruv was just chatting merrily with them in the drawing room.

"Nyra, bring some water," my father-in-law ordered.

'Why don't you bring your own ass over here and get some,' I barked in my head as I poured three glasses of water, sought the very much unused serving tray in the shelves, washed it, and went to the drawing room with a plastered smile.

"Oh, it is cold," my mother-in-law snickered. Unlike most families, I liked my mother-in-law more than my father-in-law. She was sweet, honeyed and was a devil in disguise in her own way. And she never did anything bad directly to me, she routed it through her husband….

I just pressed my lips, put up an apologetic face, glared at Dhruv, and went back to the kitchen.

"I will bring you some warm water," I heard Dhruv speak and he rushed to the kitchen.

I was still preparing tea when my phone started to buzz. It was Shlok and he was calling me on Microsoft Teams–app used by many organizations to communicate internally.

"Hello," I sighed as I pressed the phone to my ear and pulled out milk from the fridge for tea.

"Good morning, Nyra," Shlok spoke casually.

"Nothing good about this freaky morning, but how can I help," I sighed again.

"Oh, right, you are… busy… this week," he spoke with dramatic pauses.

"That I am; informed you, remember," I groaned as I added milk in the boiling water.

"Yes, I forgot, sorry, do you have five minutes?" he asked.

"Urgent or can it wait?" I demanded as I added cardamom in the tea.

"Kind of either," and I heard the scepticism in his voice, "What is wrong with you?"

"A lot of things," I groaned again. "Call you in half an hour?" I asked wondering if it was enough time to put all the niceties to end for the day.

"Sure, call me…." he sighed too.

I was about to disconnect to pour the tea in the best cups my household had, when he spoke, "And, Nyra…." he paused.

"Yes," I asked, feeling weird at his hesitation.

"Take care," he finished and disconnected.

And I smiled. Despite myself, I smiled.

I was still smiling like a fool when Dhruv came in and started putting assorted snacks in different bowls for his parents. "Tea is done?"

"Yes," I sighed, wiping the smile from my face, and lifting the tray that now held four cups.

And we left the kitchen.

Dhruv put the tray with snacks first, then took the tray from me. He gave me a very puzzled look when he placed the tray in front of his parents.

His father, a retired army officer, was busy on his phone, his mother was still talking about some aunty's daughter who was unable to find a match, and Dhruv was discussing the matter with vested interest and I felt he knew the sad poor daughter in question very well.

And I, well I just sat there, feeling like an intruder in this happy family. His father picked up a *papad* from the snack tray, chewed it absentmindedly and then picked up the cup of tea. He lifted it to his lips, sniffed it, and then screwed up his nose. He looked down at the tea, placed it back, and then shoved the tray with almighty force in my direction and spoke, "Take it back!"

I stared in shock. The tea was perfect, just the way Dhruv and I drank every day— with slight difference that it was I who had prepared it, usually Dhruv prepared the tea for me!

"Whatever you have cooked here, just take it back," his father hissed with so much anger that I flinched.

I looked between Dhruv and his mother, then scurried away with the tray in my hands.

His mother followed me and spoke, "We take tea with more milk!" She paused for a moment, and left… nothing else, she said nothing else, she just left.

And I realised that while I was talking to Shlok, I forgot to add more milk in their tea. My mistake, yes, but did I deserve the way he talked to me? Okay, I forgot, but if he had added a little more force while pushing the tray, or the tray had slipped slightly more towards me, the hot boiling tea would have fallen all over me.

As I blinked back tears, I poured a lot of milk and *malai* in the tea and boiled it.

Dhruv came to the kitchen, and I gave him my worst, 'what the fuck!' look. And to which he just said, "I told them you forgot about it, and just say sorry, it should be fine…."

And this time he ensured that there was enough milk in the tea, he strained it in the cups for them, and took them out.

They were not in the drawing room anymore. Apparently, the party had moved to their bedroom.

I slowly walked inside the room and spoke, "I am sorry, papaji," I muttered wondering why the fuck should I apologise when it was his father who almost burned me? But I said the 'right thing', which I knew *they* wanted to hear and like a good girl, I just stood there, waiting for 'his highness' to forgive me.

But he did not even look at me.

"We know you drink dark tea, but we like milk tea," my mother-in-law said with a smile. "Happens!" And she sipped the tea as she stared in space.

I sat beside Dhruv on the small sofa that we have in their room and waited. But there was absolute silence. Silence so deafening that I felt my ears would explode.

"I have calls, ma," Dhruv announced after playing on his phone for a while.

His mother nodded and he started to leave.

Finding it as cue for me too, I followed him, but his father just picked up his water bottle and raised it in my direction. Apparently, my cue was to fill the water bottle for them. And then he gestured at the tray on the bed that now had two empty cups and semi-filled snack bowls.

My mother-in-law started to pick them, but he just said, "She can take them!"

And with a smile that made my every body part ache, I nodded, and took away everything, and brought them back a water bottle filled with lukewarm water.

I was in tears, bloody tears when I reached my laptop and called Shlok. He had asked for five minutes to discuss something, and I had asked for thirty to get back. And I was almost an hour late for that call with him.

I pinged him, asking for a call.

He replied after a while with an, *Okay*, and called me.

"Free now?" he teased.

"Yes," I spoke as I swallowed the bile rising in my throat.

"The client called me this morning; they want some modifications in the proposal before going to the committee for budget approvals. I have asked Misha to take the lead, but you would need to give a sign off on it, alright?" he stressed.

"Fine," I replied.

"Also, client's budget committee will convene first Tuesday of every month, so, whenever they are ready, they want us to be there for that meeting," he continued.

"Okay," I replied again.

"But before that, we would have a lot of to-and-fro, so prepare for it," he added.

"Okay," I replied in the same robotic tone.

And this time he paused.

"Okay," he too spoke cautiously, and then spoke, "and there was an escalation on another project, so I have asked Vishal to get in touch with you. Help them while this one comes through."

"Okay," I replied again.

"What happened?" he asked finally.

"I am okay," I replied again.

"Nyra," he almost whispered my name, and I closed my eyes, finally making the tears filling my eyes slid out of them.

"Was there anything else?" I asked, controlling my sob.

He paused.

"Nothing," he replied rather curtly.

"I will talk to you later then," I tried to smile.

"Take the day off, Nyra," he insisted. "I will ask Vishal to talk to you tomorrow."

"No…." I spoke in a barely audible whisper, "Work keeps me sane!"

"Nyra…." And he whispered my name so softly this time that all I wanted to do was run and hide my face in his chest.

"Bye, Shlok."

"Bye, Nyra, take care."

And though it was not even 12 in the noon, I went to my bed and curled up in it, rocking my body to find some peace or semblance of it. Because somehow, deep down I knew, the shove to the tea tray was just the beginning. They were here just not to spend time with their son and grandchildren, they were actually here with an agenda, and I knew they were here to fight, to bring me down to my knees. And that's how my life has always been, how I have always caved in front of them for Dhruv; and I knew, no matter what I decide, I was going to lose!

7 THE COUNTDOWN... AND THEN COUNTING DOWN...

The day passed in a haze. Shlok, understanding I was suffering in some form, did not ask Vishal to talk to me and left me in peace. But at home the situation was not as peaceful.

The way they were treating me was nothing abnormal, but it was killing me. I never could understand what the fuck they wanted from me. I was obedient, well until few years ago I was even subservient to the point of slavery! I used to do everything they asked me of, literally everything. I cleaned, cooked, took care of the house, even did so many fasts—mind you no food or water kind of fasts—just because my in-laws wanted me to, and never ever asked Dhruv to lift a finger.

And yet, they were not happy. Once, crying due to the way they were treating me, I had asked my father-in-law why he was treating me in such a manner.

And to that he had said, "You don't have a filter in your mouth. You just blurt out whatever comes to your mind, and we do not appreciate it!"

That had sounded so ironic. I used to say what was on my mind, and believe me, I was never disrespectful or whatever, I always used to laugh when I used to talk to them. I talked to them like I would talk to my own parents. But then, I stopped. All of that stopped.

My said nature was my best feature before marriage. However later, they started hating me for it. And really, I do not understand why a twenty-something-year-old girl, before marriage, seems cute and bubbly to the world, and the day she gets married, she is expected to get matured and drop that cute and bubbly part of her. I mean, is marriage supposed to be like a switch for maturity? If same thing was acceptable before marriage, then why does it become unacceptable the day after marriage? Shouldn't girls be allowed to grow steadily even after marriage, should they just take all responsibilities overnight and suddenly act like a completely different person?

Anyway, I prepared lunch for everyone—a four course meal—singlehandedly. Then served them tea. Then snacks. Then fruits. Then dinner. And then tea, again. And then I retired to the bed. And oh! The wedding they were supposed to attend was mysteriously not happening. I wondered if there was a bigger purpose to their visit; not just a show of family solidarity, elders looking out for the younger ones. Were they here to ambush me? Maybe sending the kids to day care triggered it. But Dhruv had not mentioned anything to me about this. He had fallen in line with that decision happily; seemingly happily. Was he in on this? Did my husband know that his parents had entirely different agenda?

I didn't know what they wanted, but I wanted peace. And the last thing I wanted to do was fight with Dhruv because of them; something they have always wanted. And by the time my head hit the pillow, I was drained. I felt awful and super tired but when Dhruv's hand caressed my hair to check up on me, I just squeezed my eyes shut and whispered, "One day down… five more to go."

Though yesterday Shlok gave me leeway, he could not do any longer. So, today, I spent most of my morning with Vishal, understanding the project and the escalation. I immediately knew the solution to their problems, but the issue was implementation. To implement my solution, I needed to work hands-on on the project. And as the last date to resolve the issue was this Friday, I had to get my hands dirty. And so we worked. That day, I spent every minute glued to my laptop, and as I had to prepare breakfast, lunch, noon tea, snacks, fruits, evening tea and dinner, I spent most of that time in the kitchen.

Kids came home from school, they had lunch, and left for the day care… and during the time they were home, I kept the calls as less as possible. I always prioritised my kids, and even they knew it, thankfully! Dhruv understood my situation, so he helped with a few things, but God forbid if he helped in front of his parents. And that was the final straw that broke the camel's back!

The next day—day 3… only three more days left— I was in the kitchen preparing dinner while talking to Vishal about the problem in the project, when I heard raised voices from my in-laws' room.

"Vishal," I hesitated as I registered a rather high-pitched tone from my father-in-law. "Please, give me some time, I think I need to deal with something."

"Of course, ping me when you are back, Nyra," and Vishal disconnected.

I was grateful for Vishal. He was the peer I had talked to before accepting this job, and I liked this guy. He was nice, kind, a bit high-headed about what he did, but overall good. And he was very easy to get along with as well.

I tip-toed across the drawing room and heard my father-in-law say, "… why?"

I paused and wondered what they were talking about.

"Dad, it is not done," Dhruv's defeated voice came through.

"Myra did it, isn't it?" my father-in-law hissed.

And my heart thudded upon hearing Myra's, my elder sister's, name. What did she have to do with anything?

"It is not the same, dad," Dhruv sighed.

"Myra took a sabbatical, didn't she, why can't your wife do it? Even her sister knew where her priorities lie, and she…" and my father-in-law hissed, "… she does not know at all. Even though she has two children to take care of."

"Dad, Nyra took sabbatical after Shiv was born, and she was miserable. I cannot ask her to endure that again!" Dhruv spoke, and I felt relief that at least my husband was supporting me.

But his father was not having it!

"Miserable," his father scathed, "she was miserable taking care of her children and husband. What kind of a woman is she?"

'The best kind', I would have argued, 'the one that stands on her feet', but my husband instead said, "I don't dictate her decisions. She makes her own choices."

"And not to mention, she picked up that pathetic hobby of writing during that sabbatical!" his father continued in the same tone.

"She is a brilliant writer, dad," Dhruv defended me.

"Whatever may be, I am not going to read what she writes. I had read a few pages before, I was revolted by her thinking," his father raged on, and I groaned.

I never wanted his father to even read a page of what I wrote. I sadly wondered which masterpiece he had picked! Hopefully not the one that was about a sex deprived wife, who ends up hooking up with her smoking hot Brit client!

I had actually written that book to show Dhruv what could happen if he continued to keep me sex deprived and on the edge all the time. When I had published it, I had said, 'such things can happen'. But nada! He read through the book, maybe changed for a day or two, and then, it was the same sob story again....

"Her stories are imaginations," Dhruv continued in my defence.

"Anyway, why is she still working," his father continued.

"Because she has worked very hard to build herself a career," Dhruv countered, and my heart swelled at his words. "And whatever she chooses to do is her choice. I am not going to make the choice for her!"

"You are—" and I could not hear what his father said to him but there was a long silence in the room.

"Have you seen the state of your house?" his father added.

And I looked around. The house was in perfect condition, not even a speck of dust was in any corner.

"What do you mean?" Dhruv asked, confused too.

"Your kids are barely home. Have you noticed that they stay here only to sleep?" his father hissed again. "What kind of mother is she; she cannot even keep her children home. It would be better if we took them with us. At least they would get the home they deserve."

And my heart broke at these words. They have been asking to take Shiv with them ever since he was born. I still remember them asking for him every two or so months. And when Ojha was born, they were hellbent on taking him. But I had outright refused. Well, not to their faces but to Dhruv. How dare did they even think of taking my child! They never participated in his life. They only video called my kids once per day, and we send them pics every morning when they go to school. And just by doing this, they believe they can provide a better home to our children? Better than their own parents? How dare they!

I was about to march in the room and give them a piece of my mind, but Dhruv said firmly, "That won't happen, dad, so it would be good if you dropped it!"

And it looked like the matter was dropped.

"I want to talk to Nyra," his father continued.

"I do not think that is wise, dad," Dhruv intervened. "She is already stressed, I do not wish to worry her or bother her more!"

"Exactly," and without any further ado, his father bellowed, "Nyra…!"

And I jumped to my heels. Because no matter what happens, last thing I wanted to do was to get into bed that night with his father's words ringing in my ears and his cruel intentions dangling over my head. But I knew I have to face it, face them up front. So, I heaved a sigh, went back to the kitchen to turn off the stove on which today's menu was simmering, and walked back to what felt like my inevitable doom, counting down days in my head and chanting, 'Three more days to go… three more days…"

8 JUST BEING OKAY!

I walked in the room with my head held high. The moments during which I rushed to the kitchen and came back, I had made up my mind– I won't let them walk all over me; the way they have been doing for almost a decade and a half.

"Yes, papaji," I addressed his father. "You need anything?" I asked like an obedient daughter-in-law. Oh! did I say daughter-in-law, I should have said live-in maid because this man here does not even keep his used whiskey glass in the sink, and mostly makes me do all his chores!

"I want you to sit down and talk to us," he spoke in such a soft tone that despite myself my eyebrows arched up. I sat on the sofa next to Dhruv and felt him stiffen.

I wanted to tell Dhruv that it was fine, but defiance was boiling in my veins and while I appreciated him supporting me this time, I could not appreciate him leaving me high and dry in the past years. I could never forget how his parents have, without even using the exact words, stopped my visits to Jaipur—where my parents lived. How they had forced me to be the ideal Indian *bahu.* How they dressed me up as a show doll even though they knew my health condition was awful… well, those were the days in the past. I was now a rebel, or so I hoped!

And I am not saying I have been the perfect daughter-in-law. Well, I know for sure that I have committed many mistakes, and I am sure they must have not liked them. But instead of discussing it with me in a mature way, they have always kept it inside them. They never told me that with love and consideration, what I could do better. No, instead they have lashed out and passed rude, taut comments, which is never good and appreciated. Especially by a person like me!

"Yes, papaji," I asked politely.

"How are you doing?" he started.

And my eyebrows hiked up even more. The man has been treating me like his personal servant for the three fucking days and now he is asking me this!

"I am doing great," I smiled.

"But Dhruv says you are very stressed," he continued, now arching a brow himself.

"Of course, I get tired. I have two children and too many responsibilities, but I manage. We–" and I pointed at Dhruv and myself, "manage."

"Do you know why we gave you so much money last year?" he demanded.

I have never been the one who coveted their money. They must be rich, but Dhruv and I make decent money on our own. Of course, he, my father-in-law, inherited a lot of money from his father, so he was filthy rich. But well, considering our own combined earnings, we were good too.

"To help us repay the house loan," I nodded. I wanted to say so much to that, but I did not. I never liked to stoop low to other people's level; well, not until they hit me below the belt. And his next words, well, kind of felt like a hit way below the belt!

"And to ensure you do not waste time working and doing other things and focus on your children—our grandchildren—and your husband. That you do your duty as a wife and a mother and not go around looking like this–"

and he pointed at me from top to toe, "and ignore your duties to this house!"

"Dad!" Dhruv interjected but one look from his father and he quailed, turning quiet.

"How do I look exactly?" I demanded, wondering what the fuck was wrong with me. I looked okayish! I hoped.

"Like you are a young free bird," he scoffed.

Wow! Do I really look so young? I think I would take it as a compliment.... But alas, I did not say so. Instead, I asked, "And why do you think that?"

"You—" and he gave a rogue laughter that made Dhruv hiss. "You do not put *sindoor,* no *bindi,* no bangles, toe rings, nothing... you are walking and talking like you have no husband. Like you are deliberately enticing interest of other men!"

It was a slap to my face! Had he forgotten the days when I used to obey them to their very last command?

It was three years ago, post having Ojha, we had gone down to Lucknow to visit them. I was very tired with managing two children—Shiv was four and Ojha had just turned one. And I had forgotten to put *sindoor.* I had done it all, *bindi,* bangles, toe rings, even rings on my finger and *mangal sutra,* basically all the tell-tale signs of a married woman, but I had forgotten *sindoor,* I was so fucking tired.

And this man did not see how tired I was, how sleep deprived I was.... He made me sit at the dining table, served me tea and had spoken, "You act like you are a widow."

I was dumbstruck that day.

He had continued by saying, "I am ashamed to have a daughter-in-law like you, you look like you want to attract attention of other men...."

And when I had stammered and asked why he was saying that, he told me because I left out the *sindoor.*

The fucking *ek chutki sindoor* that always adorned his perfect wife's forehead!

And when I had gotten up and tried to leave, he had warned me to not pass on this encounter to my parents, and that he was incredibly displeased that I was leaving without dismissal.

Of course, I had just apologised at the moment, but in my head some other words were blasting off. Displeasure my ass, now you will see what the fuck I am going to do.

And that was the last day I had tried to act like a married woman. And it has been three years since I have adorned myself with any of those artefacts without my own will.

I just stared at him, and a yawn, a bloody yawn escaped my lips at the very moment. And this time he knew I would not care!

"Nyra," my mother-in-law intervened, "I have told you before, I don't care about these things, but he does. So even if not in front of me, but in front of your father-in-law at least, you should take care of all of this."

"I remember you saying that, yes," I nodded politely.

"And?" my father-in-law demanded.

"Okay," was all I said. Though I kept the rest of the words in my head, which were on the lines of, 'Okay, I heard you, but it is gonna happen only over my dead body, and considering I won't have control over my dead body, I think I would be fine!'

But my one worded reply made my father-in-law believe that he was winning. So, he added, "We gave you all the money so that you can live freely."

"I do live freely," I shrugged.

"And you take care of your children," he stressed.

"I do take care of my children, I am their mother. And no one… I mean no one can care for them more than I do!"

"So, where are they?" he demanded.

"Enjoying a merry time playing with their friends in a safe environment," I chirped.

"They are not home," he growled.

"Considering what is happening here right now, I do not think their home is a safe environment at present," I replied, but in a much, *much* softer tone.

His eyes glared with rage.

"We are telling you one last time, you have to stop working," he declared. "No woman in our house works, except for you." He spat the word 'you'. "And your husband earns enough to give you a good life. So, why do you even have to work!"

"Because I like to work," I replied simply.

"But you do not like to work at home," he barked. "You do not like to teach your kids, make them good food, spend time with them!"

"You are wrong, but whatever I may say, you won't change your thoughts, so I am not going to argue!" I sighed.

"Look at Myra!" he dragged my sister again.

"Let's keep my sister out!" I growled despite myself. They did not know the bloody truth about my sister, and I really did not wish to tell them in such mood!

"Stop working, Nyra," he ordered this time, with a hidden 'or else' in the end.

"Okay," I spoke simply. And even Dhruv's head snapped in my direction.

Everyone was shocked with my obedience.

Maybe he was emboldened by my submission, because he continued, "And I want you to stop writing. You don't need freelance work or whatever meagre job you do! I just want you to focus on your children and husband."

"Okay," I repeated in the same simple tone. The rage was filling inside me. Stop writing! Who the fuck he thinks of himself? I write to keep my sanity, I started writing when I was going through the worst phase of my life, and it was my writing that brought me out of that pit. Writing brought me clarity, it brought me peace and sanity. It provided me an outlet to ease the building pain. And he wants me to stop writing! Holy fuck!

"That is all," he spoke, still unsure of what just happened. Because I wanted to tell him what the fuck had just happened! But I just stayed put.

"Great," I patted my thighs with my hands, they were shaking with fury that I was keeping at bay. "Dinner is ready, why don't you two eat it while it is still warm, and Dhruv and I will go and pick up the kids."

"See you need him to go everywhere, you call yourself independent, but you are not. You are so dependent on him!" he scathed.

"Okay," I repeated, now my calm façade cracking.

"Let's go," Dhruv spoke as he grabbed my elbow and dragged me out. He knew the dam of my patience was about to break and he literally wanted me out of the house before that happened.

And the moment I stepped out the house, in the elevator, it exploded. I slapped, punched, kicked every part of Dhruv I could reach, and he let me. The only thing I did not do was slap him on the face, but his chest, stomach, back, arms, legs… all were my victims today. We descended ten floors during which time he let me hit him. Why? I do not know… maybe he knew I needed to vent out, or maybe he knew he deserved every hit I was giving him. How dare he not defend me? How dare he not utter a single word to his father? How dare he not stand up for me?

As we picked up the kids, I tried my best to keep my tears at bay because I did not want my children to know what shit went down. We came back home, had our dinner and then quietly retired for the day.

In my room, I realised that Dhruv did not explain or apologise for *his* behaviour at all. Yes, he defended me slightly when he felt I was not listening, but in front of me, he let his father walk all over us, and he even forced me to bend over backwards to his father's whims.

But before filling the room with his all too familiar snores, he simply told me to do whatever shit I wanted to do and ignore his father's words. They would come around eventually.

But would they? And as I went to bed, staring at my kids—I had forgotten about the promise I had made to Vishal—I knew if I have to survive, if I have to live, if I have to stay sane, I need to start fighting for myself like I have always done. Just being 'Okay' or saying 'Okay' would not work. Because just like in my childhood, no one was going to come to my rescue. I needed to fight for my happiness. And if not for me, then for my kids. They needed a sane mother. They needed a happy mother, and presently, their mother was incredibly unhappy and depressed. And from experience I knew, a depressed and unhappy mother ruins entire life of her children, even if unintentionally. So, I know I need to step up, I need to stay stable, and for that, I need to stand up for myself. But when would that happen? Well, only time would tell.

9 NEW TUNE FOR MY BROKEN MIND!

I could not sleep at all, of course, and it broke my already clobbered mind further. And it resulted in hysterical sobs through the night and even in the morning.

No one asked me why I had sore and red eyes in the morning; my in-laws just treated me like I was dressed in my pink princess dress and was there to serve and please. They, however, were super energetic that morning. But no matter how I felt, I prepared the breakfast and talked down Shiv when he asked to stay back from tuition to spend time with his grandparents. I promised him to bring him back home early today, the moment he would finish his studying. And he was very happy with the prospect.

But this promise also earned me a snort from my in-laws. And it was this snort, and my already tired and feverish body, that forced me to walk back to my room and sob a little more. They knew I had been crying but they did not care. No one cared in the house, well, I could not say anything about Dhruv as he had to leave very early that day for an important meeting. And because I was in some sleepless stupor at that time, I could not wave him goodbye.

Ironically, his parents did not like that too. Oh, their poor son had to prepare his own morning tea and had to prepare a glass of warm milk for me too. Oh, their poor son had to do so much with his own two hands, because his live-in maid was out cold! Oh, fuck you!

I dropped the kids to school, they felt I was upset because they hugged me extra-long when they waved me goodbye, and I came back to the place which was supposed to be my safe haven but currently was a hellhole for me!

I prepared the breakfast for them in silence. And on the side, I also prepared the lunch. I really did not wish to stay in the kitchen, in their doleful presence, for any longer than absolutely necessary.

I stayed in my room for very long, not daring to even open my laptop because I knew I would make some mistake if I started to work. I stayed curled up in my bed when my phone started to ring. I was hoping it was Dhruv, asking about my wellbeing since I simply had ignored his message that had stated he had reached office and a second one sometime later asking, if I had dropped the kids to school. But it was Vishal.

"Hello," I tried to speak in as normal voice as I could conjure.

"Some people just forget their promises. I know it is my project and it is my ass on the line, but I thought you were my friend," Vishal grunted in annoyance.

"Sorry," I choked.

"Sorry for ditching me or what? I don't understand what you mean?" he barked.

"Sorry," and I started sobbing. "I am sorry, I did not mean to…" and I cried so bitterly that there was absolute quiet on the other side.

This was all just too much for me. Dhruv's ignorance, my in-laws' treatment, their demands, and now Vishal's harsh words and attitude. It was just too much for me.

I pushed the phone on the bed and continued to cry for what seemed like hours.

The phone buzzed again, I hiccupped myself to stop, and spoke, "Sorry, it was unprofessional of me," I sniffed.

"Just shut up with professionalism and tell me what happened," Vishal demanded.

"Nothing," I choked.

"Nyra," he threatened.

"Nothing happened, absolutely nothing happened." And I thought of Dhruv, how he betrayed me, how he does not even touch me to calm my sadness, how–how in fact, nothing ever happens in my life.

"Nyra," and his tone softened.

"I have thought of the solution to your problem," I spoke, stifling more sobs.

"I don't give a fuck about my project right now, okay," Vishal started.

"Work helps," I choked again, and then relayed the solution to him.

He was dumbfounded.

"How, I mean how!" he was speechless.

"How what?" I asked, surprised, as I hiccupped again. "I can code it for you if you like. Though I think I will make some mistakes at present."

"I mean how are you able to think about it when you are so sad?" he asked in a perturbed tone.

"Work helps, I will talk to you later," and without any answer from him, I disconnected the call.

I cried for another two hours or so, when my phone buzzed again. I was so upset, so devastated, that I had ignored Dhruv's calls too. I did not wish to talk to him at the moment. I did not wish to talk to anyone at the moment.

But despite myself, I checked the message, and it was a text from Shlok.

It was just one word, *Hi.*

I wiped my nose on my pillowcase, and blurry eyed replied, *Hi.*

How are you? he asked.

Fine, I lied.

Working? he continued.

No, not able to.

Why? and I felt he was going to scold me for skipping work. But then more words popped up on my screen, *Are you not well?*

Not well! which was partial truth.

Want to talk about it? he asked. And why did I feel he knew that my illness was not physical but emotional.

Not as of now! I replied.

I will be in office tomorrow, see you then? he offered.

And now I felt he really knew about my situation, or he knew of it!

I cannot, this week is kind of weird for me.

And another tear streamed down my cheek, damn! I was missing meeting him, and for who? My in-laws!

Why? he asked again.

And this time I gave in.

My in-laws are here, I cannot come, I replied honestly.

And there was silence then. He had read the message, the two blue ticks said as much, but he did not reply.

Is it why you are so upset these days? he asked after a long pause.

I cannot say! I sighed.

I have meetings next week, but see you next Friday? he offered.

I can be in office next Friday, yes.

Great, and, Nyra, take the rest of the week off and take care!

And it was those two words in the end that said it all. I saw other messages on my WhatsApp saying Dhruv was on his way back and he would pick up the kids from school. So, I decided to turn the phone off and close my eyes to sleep.

And as I went to bed during the day, my routine upset thoroughly now, I did not know what the fuck I was supposed to do. This breakdown was killing me. And while the daunting words of my in-laws were playing in my head on a constant loop, another tune had also started playing in my broken mind. The tune that had the lyrics of the messages from Shlok, and it played in my head in his voice. And while nothing else calmed me down, it was his voice that day that had dried up my tears and slowly lulled me to sleep.

SOME GOOD THING! 10

I woke with a laughter ringing in my head. And as I registered the sound of that laugh, I realised it was not coming from outside, but from within me. And that it did not resemble the laugh of anyone I was currently living with—i.e., my husband or father-in-law—but then of whom? But no matter how hard I tried to put a face to this laughter, I could not.

Still pondering over the same, I stepped out of the room to check if Shiv and Ojha had eaten lunch and if they had left for tuition. It was 5 PM now, and they should be in day care to study. But much to my shock, they were playing carrom with their grandparents.

"You are up," Dhruv smiled as he looked up from his laptop.

Dhruv and I had a system. One of us always stayed present with the kids when they were home. So, it meant, only one of us ever took calls at one point of time, well, calls that require silence in the background. And whoever took the important call, took it from the room, where kids were not allowed during meetings, and the other person worked from the living room, supervising the kids in the process.

"You guys had lunch?" I asked Shiv and Ojha. They nodded happily as Shiv targeted the queen on the board with a wild glee in his eyes.

"Your mother-in-law had to prepare the *chapatis* while you slept in the day," my father-in-law scowled.

"Okay," I replied. "I did the dough, I made the dal and veggie, she made the *chapatis*; so I think it is okay!" I spoke curtly, I was so done with the drama.

And before he could reply, I turned my gaze over to Dhruv and said, "And why are they not in tuition?"

"We made them do their homework," and my father-in-law pointed at their bags. "Not that difficult to teach if you stay awake," and he snorted.

"Dhruv, you know it is not just homework that a 3rd standard student needs to do, hell, even 1st standard student needs wider study plan. Why did they not go today," I demanded.

"Mom," Shiv spoke in a soft tone.

"What?" I started to snap but stopped. It was not his fault; he was the innocent flower in the middle of these thorns.

"I did not wish to go today. They are leaving tomorrow, so–"

And the words 'leaving tomorrow' had such an excellent calming impact on me that I just smiled at my son.

"You did all the homework?" I asked him seriously.

And he nodded and started narrating some really farfetched stories from school.

"And Ojha did hers too?" I demanded.

While Ojha smiled lovingly at me, Shiv complained about her handwriting.

"You have to go tomorrow to tuition, alright?" I insisted.

And both my children nodded and went back to carrom.

"What would you like to have for dinner tonight?" I asked the room in general. But nobody responded. So I turned to Dhruv and spoke, "Dhruv, I am not feeling too well today. Let us have pasta tonight."

And while both the kids started celebrating that they would have pasta, I turned around and left the room without sparing another look to any of the adults in the room, who I know were staring at me.

Dhruv came in my room a little later and asked if I needed anything. He even brought my kind of tea with him, which helped lift my mood a bit.

"Your parents are awful," I complained as I sipped the tea.

"I know, but well, parents," he shrugged.

"Your parents, your problem, you deal with them," I sighed.

"I know," he shrugged again.

"Did you realise they never went to that supposed 'wedding'," I growled.

"I did realise that," he nodded.

"If they wanted to ambush me, they could have done it directly. I would never say no to their coming here, Dhruv, despite whatever they do to me! Why did they lie?" I asked seriously.

"I will talk to them," he started, but as I narrowed my eyes at him, he added, "… about everything. They will stop behaving like this, I promise," he assured me. And then planting a soft kiss on my forehead, he left.

Shiv, Ojha and I had pasta to fill our bellies, and Dhruv and his parents had their standard 'Dal Makhani, Paneer and assorted breads'. Everyone was happy, especially me because I absolutely love pasta.

While we ate, the kids talked a lot. But I could sense tension in the house. I could feel daggers shooting in my direction every so often, and by the end of dinner, I felt I was thoroughly sliced, but I relented.

I put kids to bed, and then made my way to where Dhruv and his parents were talking. I slumped on the chair near them, knowing it would be best for them to vent out whatever shit they had piling in their head, and braced myself.

The moment I sat down, his father spoke, "I hear you are not going to heed any of my words from before."

"Okay," I replied like a broken record.

This word now infuriated him more.

"Listen here, Nyra," he started, and I just stared at him. "You leave this job and start doing your duties as a mother and wife, or…"

"Or what?" I asked now, rather coldly.

"Or we would never come and live with you in this house again."

Dhruv countered his words, threats were passed, displeasure was sounded, but it felt to me I was floating away. Why would I even care to do something that would bring them back here? Okay, yes, they were Dhruv's parents, but so what? When have they ever done anything good for me, his wife, their supposed daughter? And yes, I know, they absolutely love my children… but wasn't me, the kids' mother worth a damn?

So no, I did not react. I did not utter any words of apologies. I did not even show them that how bad it would be if they decided to never darken my doorstep. No, I just stayed put and let their son deal with the situation.

And as we went to bed that night, Dhruv really worried now, I knew at least a good thing would happen—no, no… no, no… I *hoped* for a good thing that could happen out of all this shit. Maybe, perhaps maybe, I won't have to live with them again. And as for my husband and kids, they are more than welcome to go and live with them for a few days in Lucknow. I was all but fine on two conditions– firstly, they never dragged me with them when they visited Lucknow, and secondly, they come back to me… that they always come back to me.

11 A FIRST FOR EVERYTHING

The next week passed in a haze of silence and work. I really did not wish to talk to Dhruv, or even look at him. He had been so awful when his father demanded such things from me. I mean, who the fuck was he to even ask all that? Why did they even marry their son to an ambitious girl? Yes, I was stupid, naïve when I married Dhruv, but were they also as stupid and naïve as I was? Did they not see how vibrant, how hard working and how dedicated I was towards my work? After all, it was them who had chosen me….

Many many years ago, when Dhruv and I were working in Chandigarh on a project, where he was the client lead, his parents had visited him. You know, just to meet him, see how he was doing, how he was living! And they had met me.

Dhruv and I were never dating, but we were best friends. A friendship that was brewing in my heart back then, and even then, I knew I was madly and deeply in love with him, but I always kept my feelings in check. So did he because he never expressed anything, hell, he had never even held my hand till then. He just took care of me, made sure I was fine and provided me moral support. And while I did not need his protection per se, I needed moral support because I always kept on landing in some trouble or the other, sometimes with some guy who wanted my attention or sometimes with a co-worker—mainly his other friends—who loathed me for stealing his attention within such short span of time.

Anyway, his parents came and met a few of his friends, and me! And I don't know what they saw, maybe the same thing that all his friends saw to give me such horrible treatment every so often, that his father took a liking to me. His father made sure to spend a lot of time with me on his visit, and by the end of that week, he asked Dhruv to propose to me and ask for marriage. He even sat me down and said, "Our Dhruv loves you a lot, and while we are seeking a good girl for him outside, if you are up for it, we would like you to be that girl."

Dhruv was dead silent back then too. I had just stared at him at this announcement. Did Dhruv really love me? He never said anything, but he just shrugged in a gesture that I knew meant, 'Well, I can, if you are up for it.'

And then, well, a lot of things had happened. My parents were called, my father did not like the idea of marrying me off at the age of 21– I was 21 when all this started, and he claimed that it was the reason and not that Dhruv was eight years older than I was, but then my mom convinced him and the date for our marriage was set.

In all of this, no one said the words, 'You would have to stop working when you bear our grandchildren' or that, 'You would be a free live-in maid to our son and our entire family for the rest of your life'.

Because had they said all this, had I truly known what marrying in Manchanda household meant, I would have had a much, much different future. And while I loved Dhruv to my core, I always will, he was the perfect father and man any girl could dream of; his silence and no-reaction attitude just does not sit well with me.

The Friday came, and while I did not bother checking with Shlok if he would come down to the office as he had promised, I planned it with Vishal. Vishal went to office daily as he lived close to the office premises. Vishal had been with Polar Technologies for his entire career, but I was not one bit surprised that he had spent fifteen years of his life in the same company, well, people do stay loyal if the organization did too.

Anyway, I booked a cab for office and left. Dhruv was already in his office. The dynamics of my household had changed, but the schedule had not wavered. I was still taking care of the children, talking to Dhruv for all important matters, he was replying as if nothing had happened, but something had happened. My heart was broken by the betrayal from his side, and why did I feel that he did not even realise it. That he hurt me, that he had made me upset. I knew he has been taking me for granted for years, but has he been taking me so much for granted that his father said so much to me and he did not even bother to show some affection to make sure I was okay after all the shit!

Tears pooled in my eyes again as the cab drove towards the office.

I reached the office at 11AM, thanks to the horrible Delhi traffic and pressed the number 4 elevator button to reach the floor. I scanned myself in the elevator mirror, I was wearing black knee length pencil skirt, white tucked in shirt and flat shoes. I know on a dress like this, heels would look elegant and sexy as fuck, but I cannot wear heels. I cannot wear any uncomfortable shoes. Hell, I cannot stay on my feet for a very long time.

I checked my face and fixed my hair again, they were getting unruly, again. The solemn sadness was etched in my eyes, and I could not help but notice the downward tilt of my lips. I always stay happy, always smiling. No matter the scenario, I laugh because deep down I know my life was a horrible shit, and if I don't laugh all the time, the world would see, hell, I would see what shit I live in.

But today, that fake laugh also was eluding me.

Anyway, I perked my lips up, blinked back the sadness shadowing my eyes—at least tried to—and walked in the office.

There were around fifty people there, and all strangers.

First one I saw was Vishal. He was standing at a distance and talking to someone animatedly. I waved at him as I tried to find my newly allocated seat. I wonder why that was even necessary when people hardly came to office. I mean, I am here after almost three months of joining this organization and did not know when next I would be there!

Vishal found me as I settled on my desk, and then dragged me to show around, introducing me to people I did not know. But I found his friends to be good. They were approachable and friendly. I talked to a few of them, spent time with others, but there was that lingering sadness that kept on hitting me every so often. A feeling that kept on recoiling like the snap of a rubber band insisting that I was not a deserver of this distraction, this momentary forgetting of my true situation, that I was doomed forever. And every time this hit came, the people around me asked "What's wrong? Are you okay?" and it was not that snap or hit of sadness that kept on flooding me, but the question, that forced me to swallow the rising bile and shake my head and smile. Because in no way, no fucking way I was going to air my dirty laundry to this group of strangers.

I even met a few of Vishal's team members. In the past week I had been working very closely with them, and they all were all smiles when we met. I sat and worked with them until 3PM when someone tapped my desk.

I looked up and found Shlok. I do not know why, but my face lit up with the first genuine smile when I saw him. While my face always lights up at the mention of his mere name—I always try to curl back that smile to not show that I have a soft spot for that devil—but today, with him beaming down at me, I could not help but light up like a bulb.

"You are here," he smiled, his smile so damn genuine that I let myself feast on it for a few seconds.

"I am here," I replied, unable to stop myself. And I noticed him for the first time. Strange, I did not notice his physical aspects when we met back in Bangalore, but today, as he stood next to my desk, I noticed how tall he was, maybe an inch or two taller than me but tall–well, I was around five eight! I noticed how his muscular chest showed well from his perfect fitted shirt, and how his stomach was a little bulgy, not the beer-belly kind that so many men bore with pride, but just a little. His hair was neatly done, and his beard seemed to be recently trimmed. All in all, he looked good!

"And you are late, fashionably so!" I continued before my thoughts made the pause awkward.

And his laughter boomed in the surroundings.

Fuck! This was it. For the past five days, I have been waking up to the sound of a laughter. Not a manic laughter, but a laughter that was so carefree and happy that the sound of it was the only bright moment in my otherwise awfully bleak last week. And for the five days I have been trying to place who was the source of that beautiful laughter, and now it hit me.

It was Shlok! Damn, I have been waking up to Shlok's laughter for five mornings.

"What?" he asked quizzically as he found me staring at him in shock.

"Nothing," I shook my head.

"Talk?" he asked, now concern filling his face.

And the happiness and smiles that had bubbled in me at his appearance faded.

"Okay," I whispered.

But his phone dinged.

"Shit!" he cursed, "I forgot!" and he gave me a fleeting look.

"You have a meeting that you forgot about?" I asked with raised eyebrows.

He scrunched his nose and nodded.

"Find me when you are available, I am free this afternoon," I smiled at him, and he nodded again.

But he did not find me again. He was busy… on some calls, with other people, and, I did not understand what I was feeling at the sight, with one other girl in particular.

Around sixish, when I was looking to book the cab to head back home, Vishal found me.

"What's up?" Vishal asked casually.

"Back home, what else?" I smiled again.

"Are you really okay?" Vishal asked yet again.

"I am better now, getting out of the house helped," I nodded.

"Good, so this would make you feel even better, a group of us are going to play poker at Shlok's house, join us," Vishal ordered. Yes, he did not ask, he did not request, he just ordered.

"I don't know anything about a poker game," I spoke as my eyes fell on Shlok, who was again talking to that same girl!
"Who is she?" I asked as I tilted my head in their direction.

"Grisha, another oldie in the company," Vishal smiled. These oldies, or as Vishal referred to people who have stayed more than ten years in Polar Technologies, were very close friends.

"So, poker game?" Vishal asked again.

"Should it not be the host who should invite me? I do not go anywhere without a proper invite," I rolled my eyes, trying damn hard to remove the itch from within me. Shlok called me here, and yet he did not invite me to a game hosted at his house!

"I just invited you," Vishal sighed.

"At someone else's house!" I retorted.

"Wait here," and he left.

I just shook my head and continued to stare at the map on my laptop, wondering when I should call for a cab. When someone tapped the desk.

"Hi, Nyra," Shlok spoke.

"Hello," and I smiled again.

"I am sorry, got caught up!"

And I just wondered where! It was the first time I had come to this office, and these people don't do any work here. All they do is roam around, talk to random people, and spend time in game room. Only a handful of people take some occasional calls….

"By the way, Vishal told you right, join us for poker night," Shlok invited.

"I–" I hesitated. I knew it was Vishal who had asked him to invite me, and Shlok did not really want me there.

"Oh, come on… join me. I am leaving right now! You can come with me, we can talk on the way, while others join us at my place," he insisted.

And I thought about it. It was not a very difficult decision really! I knew Dhruv had freed his evening to pick up the kids, and he anyway was going to order in because post my day in office, we both knew I won't be able to cook any dinner. So, what was there to lose? Maybe this small poker night will help bring some sanity to me.

And just like that, I nodded.

"Great, let's go," and he walked back to a seat, two rows down, and picked up his packed bag, showing he was all ready to go. I quickly did the same and followed him, muttering to Vishal on the way that I would find him in Shlok's house. To which he nodded.

Last night, after another gloomy day, when Dhurv and I had gone to bed, I had thought a lot about what I would say to Shlok… what I would tell him so that my life, at least from work front, could stay manageable. I had even considered asking him about a sabbatical to gain some sanity, but in all my imaginations, I had not thought about going to Shlok's house, to play poker! Well, there is always first for everything, and this was mine…

12 SMALL ACTION GARNERS BIG REACTION!

We rode in silence for a while, where he asked me some random questions, and I just answered them. One of my favourite songs was playing, *Ae dil hai mushkil,* on FM and I found it so ironic for it to play out of all the possible songs. The lyrics were so to the point for my situation that I just smiled at them.

"What's on your mind?" Shlok asked seriously.

"Nothing," I sighed.

"And that says it all, that sigh, it is more than enough for me to know something is not right," Shlok added grimly.

"My in-laws were here," I chewed my lips.

"And?" Shlok encouraged me to speak.

"I mean, I am a bad mother, I know it," I started.

He was driving, but I knew he blinked in surprise at my words as he interjected, "I do not think you are a bad mother!"

"I know I am not the best mother," I rolled my eyes.

"You are the best version of yourself, I can tell that," Shlok insisted. "I have heard you talk about your children on the calls we have had, you are not a bad mother, Nyra," he stressed the last words.

And a wave of relief flooded over me. Because I have said these words, like a lot, in my home in front of Dhruv, but never, not even once, had he said that I was 'not a bad mother'. Dhruv never said anything, he neither agreed nor denied, like he always does, he stayed quiet, which assured me that I, in fact, was not a good mother.

"What gave you the idea you are a bad mother, though?" Shlok asked seriously.

And I studied his face, his eyes were glued to the road, but he was giving me side glances.

"My in-laws," I started again, and this time he just nodded. "I do not take care of my children as much as I used to, I have sent them to day care, to tuition, I sometimes am not even able to cook for them…"

"All this your in-laws said or your husband?" Shlok asked seriously.

"Oh, Dhruv does not say a word, honestly. He just listens, and at times, I doubt he even does that. He just stares in the space, looks at his phone, shrugs, but does not speak up a lot," I informed.

"But you–" and a grin appeared on Shlok's face.

"Exactly, I cannot even stay quiet to save my own life," I laughed. And this time he gave me a long fleeting look before looking back at the road again.

"Like they say, opposites attract," Shlok grinned.

"Touche!" I nodded.

"But, Nyra," Shlok spoke seriously now, "what you do, however much you do, is more than enough. You love your kids, you take care of them, you protect them, you make sure they are safe…"

"But…"

"No buts, what does it matter you are not able to teach them? Didn't you tell me the other day that you are happy they go to day care because now they are playing with their friends and enjoying, like a lot!"

"That's true," I nodded.

"And they study there too. Tell me this. Is the place where they go safe?" he asked.

"Actually, the day care is run by Shiv's old teacher, and I trust her a lot," I stressed.

"So, you are taking care of their studies, their playtime, and their security, what else do you want?"

"And by being there, their screen time is also very less now," I smiled to myself.

"And you were harbouring thoughts that you are a bad mother for sending them there," he chuckled lightly, and I felt relieved.

We were sitting in traffic when he asked again, "And you cook yourself? Why do you not hire a cook to do it for you?"

"Because," I shrugged, "Shiv won't eat if a cook makes it. Once in a while is fine, but he stops eating if it is not prepared by me."

Shlok did not respond to this. And I knew why, it was because I had taken Shiv's name. If I had given any other reason, he would have argued!

We spent rest of the ride talking about him. He was the eldest child, had a younger sister and brother too. The sister lived in Noida, while the brother lived with his parents in Meerut. None of them were married, and while they were searching for a suitable groom for his sister, they were yet to find one.

"And why have you not gotten married yet?" I asked, intrigued.

"Because I did not find the right person yet," he smiled.

And his words made my smile falter.

"What's wrong?" he asked seriously.

"Finding the right person is crucial, yes," I replied solemnly.

"And you found him," he grinned.

I took a moment to reply. Yes, I had found Dhruv, and he was the perfect gentleman, but was he the perfect gentleman for me? Yes, he loved me, but so many times I felt his love for me was not as a partner but that of a father! He cared for me, he adored me, he took care of my all needs, but—but he never touched me. He never did anything to make my heart flutter. And he never, not unless I asked him to, had sex with me! Which rarely happened because, well, a girl can only ask as much....

"Huh!" Shlok asked curiously as we drove into a gated society.

"Of course," I sighed, and he chuckled.

"Hey, not fair!" I spoke dramatically as he laughed.

"I did not say a thing," he laughed again.

Ignoring his chuckle that held a lot of meaning, I looked around. "Your parking area reminds me of my time in Mumbai. We lived in a similar society back then, the parking was a maze there too," I commented as he just kept on driving in the parking lot to reach his own parking space.

"Yeah, took me a while to remember the path," he nodded seriously. But then he hit the brakes, "Damn," and he reversed and started to drive out.

"What happened?" I asked, curiously.

"Had to buy some snacks for poker night, forgot while talking to you," and he just drove out.

We reached a mall near his house in less than ten minutes. He parked very quickly, dumped our laptop bags in the trunk of his car and started to walk. I followed at his heels and as soon as we arrived at the ground floor of the mall, where a supermarket was present, I fell back. His strides were too long and fast for me. He was yet to know my medical history, and while our heights were not that drastically different, I just could not meet his pace.

He walked ahead for like a minute or so, and then stopped and turned.

He had a mildly amused expression on his face.

"I cannot walk very fast," I murmured, always the sore subject for me. I always felt embarrassed of this fact because

I do walk rather slowly, like an old person! I was improving, significantly so… but still, it was a long road ahead for me.

"Okay," was all he said, and he fell in steps with me.

He was practically dragging his feet, humming a tune, when I said, "You can go ahead, Shlok, it is fine!"

"And why would I do that?" he asked, looking confused.

And it hit me! Dhruv never walked beside me, like never. He was quite taller than me, and hence, always took longer strides. But even before I fell ill, stopped wearing heels and started dawdling, he had never walked beside me. Every time we went out somewhere, despite me asking him a million times to walk beside me so that we could share the experience of our surroundings together, he never walked with me. He was always at least twenty steps ahead, always!

"Are you okay?" Shlok asked seriously.

"I am fine," I shook my head and stared at him.

Shlok gave me a rather quizzical look, then smiled back.

"You really need to talk to someone, you know," he muttered. And he pointed at a shop and started talking about the brands and how his favourite perfume was from the same brand.

We stepped in the supermarket, he pulled out a trolley and started filling it with required items. Out of habit, I kept on falling behind, and he kept on waiting for me. Not once he left my side. He asked me a lot of questions, discussed so many things, but never once he left my side.

And it was this action, this small action, a minuscule gesture, that forced me to think about Shlok a lot for many nights in the future every time I went to bed. I think it was his this action that filled my heart with a fuzzy warmth, making me ache for my husband, Dhruv, to stay beside me and talk to me. Spend time with me in not just silence but talk about anything and everything. That he just be with me… I think it was Shlok's this action that triggered a big reaction that kept on stirring in my brain in coming months.

13 GESTURES, BIG AND SMALL

I did not know what I was feeling when we arrived at his home. I have never been to another man's house alone before. And if it were someone else, I would not have stepped inside the door. But I trusted Shlok. I do not know why, but I trusted him so much that I did not hesitate even a bit to step inside and take in the surroundings.

"You have an incredibly beautiful house," I commented as I took off my shoes and walked inside.

"Thanks," he smiled with pride. "Let me give you a tour," and he showed me his three-bedroom apartment with a flourish, though the door to the third room was locked.

It was nicely decorated, it had good furniture, and it was clean. I mean, like surgically clean.

"Geez, I do not think my house was ever this clean," I laughed as we finally sat on the sofa set in his living room.

"I don't have kids," he smiled.

"Even when I had no kids, my house was never this clean," I remarked, again staring at the perfect living room, which resembled a lot like a show house.

"Maid does it," he just shrugged.

"Hmm, when I had no husband or kids, I could not afford a maid except for floor cleaning and dishes," I nodded.

"And that's why mine is cleaner than yours," and he grinned again. "I will go freshen up," he spoke and disappeared behind his bedroom doors.

Feeling weird and having nothing to do, I walked to the kitchen, and started unpacking the grocery he had bought. Of course, I was not a crazy lady who would just start unpacking someone else's groceries, but he had started doing it when he had showed me the kitchen and I was just finishing it for him. And while, of course, I could not put his snacks in shelves, I put the milk, curd, bottles of cold drinks, soda and juices in the fridge. I was just putting away the eggs when he came back.

"What are you doing?" he asked, surprised.

"Putting things away," I replied.

"No need," he spoke as he shoved all the snacks in a shelf haphazardly. Okay, so not that surgically clean after all, I thought bemused; in fact, this was a lot like me when I am not acting as a mom and a perfect homemaker.

"Come," and he grabbed the snacks he had picked as per my choosing, took two empty glasses, water and led me out to the balcony. "What did you want to talk about?" he asked, opening the packet of crisps, and offering it to me.

"I may resign," I dropped the bomb, and he almost dropped the bag of crisps.

"Why?" he asked after a long awkward pause.

"Too much shit!" I shook my head.

He walked back in the room and came back with a pack of cigarettes. "Mind if I?" he asked.

"Go ahead," I gestured to him as I watched him placing it on his lips and light up a stick. He finished the entire cigarette, lit another one, took a long puff, and finally looked at me.

"No, you are not resigning," he ordered.

"I—" I started but he raised his index finger and spoke, "I don't care. You are not resigning, period!"

"My family!" I groaned.

"Your husband wants you to resign?" he asked with raised eyebrows.

"I do not know what my husband wants, Shlok. He does not share a fucking thing with me. He just stays silent and does not interact with me on any point."

"Not on anything?" he demanded, now looking confused.

"He talks about basic necessities, he talks about the kids, he talks about work, he–" I trailed off, wondering how I could tell him that Dhruv and I have not spent an hour in last decade as just us… as a couple! I mean Dhruv talks to me, yes, but only about things that are required to be talked about, kids' health, their education, their requirements, if any grocery needs to be ordered, if fruits are there in the house or not, if maid is causing troubles and, etc. But never about if I want to work… if I am happy, if he is happy, if either of us want to go out and have a vacation!

"Nyra, how are you really?" Shlok asked with such sincerity that I realised that no one, literally, no one in my entire life had asked me this question. Not like they meant it…. Strangers have asked it as a customary greeting in most corporate calls, but no one in my family or friends has ever asked me this question.

"Fine," I just shrugged, and he heaved a sigh.

"May I?" I asked as I pointed at his cigarette.

"You smoke?" he asked, confused but he offered me one.

"Not in the past decade and a half," and without pausing, I just lit it and inhaled the smoke that felt like a balm to my aching soul. I exhaled the smoke through the nose and Shlok just laughed.

"I was waiting for you to get a coughing fit," he laughed again.

"Well," and I just stood in his balcony and observed the beautiful view outside. He lived on the seventh floor, and at the horizon the setting sun, and greenery that was displayed in front of us was mesmerising.

We stood there for long moments, just puffing out smoke that has killed millions of people but did not speak.

"Your house has a beautiful aura," I murmured, still staring out.

"What?" he asked, confused, and I repeated.

"Thanks," his reply was even more confused.

"I don't know if you believe it or not, but houses are entities, and they have an aura. And it varies from house to house, and also depends on the people who live in it. Yours has a beautiful aura," I smiled.

He smiled back.

"It is just clean," he shrugged.

"That it is," I chuckled lightly. "But aura is something different," and as I stared at his amused expressions, I added, "You won't understand," I grinned.

We stood in the balcony for another thirty minutes, I was chewing breath mint when other people began arriving. I was hoping for a hoard of people, considering he bought so much snacks, but there were only six people, including me and Shlok! And strangely, all guys except for me. The way he was talking to Grisha chick, the way they were laughing together, I had thought she was a must-come type participant, but apparently, she was not. At first, I felt awkward, but then I realised all of the guys were actually nice. And slowly, I opened up.

We played poker.... I neither won, nor lost, I stayed at breakeven. Why? Because I do not play blind or take risks, and I have the worst poker face. Within twenty minutes of the game, everyone knew if I am making a bet, it meant I have good cards, and all others would fold, unless they had an awesome hand! So, yeah, I stayed at breakeven, lol. But others played, and won a few, lost a few, and it was fun.

Shlok ordered light dinner, we all then ate while laughing and talking about all nonsensical things, and then me, Vishal and Shlok went to the balcony, while all others left for their homes. It was already past 10PM and Vishal promised to drop me home safely, whenever we left.

Vishal was opening up in front of me, more than ever before, and I liked this side of him as much as the other one. Shlok, being our senior, stayed a little cautious throughout, but I noticed he laughed and joked quite easily when out of office stress.

Around midnight the conversation drifted towards our partners. Vishal, as it turned out, was also struggling in his marriage, and to this my question was, "Who is not! I wonder why people even get married?"

"And that's why I am still single," Shlok laughed.

"So, what kind of girl do you want?" Vishal asked Shlok.

Shlok paused and spoke, "She needs to be beautiful, looks matter to me, though people may call it vain," he shrugged, and Vishal grinned.

I wonder what the inside joke was!

"She should be very smart, passionate and should keep things interesting in my life."

"You have a very vague definition of the girl you want," I laughed.

"And oh," Shlok spoke quickly, like he remembered something important, "she should add value to my home."

And when I stared at him, wondering that if he too believed that girls should be stuck caring for their homes, he added, "I mean, I do not want her to do all the chores in the house, but she should help me manage it well."

"So smart, passionate, interesting and homey," I summarised, "And beautiful."

"Very beautiful, yes," Shlok nodded.

"So, you are out of the question, Nyra," Vishal mocked me, and I felt a jolt.

Was I even in the running here? I wondered, but instead I asked, abashed, "Hey, what is wrong with me?"

"Just that your number won't come," Vishal continued in his mock tone.

And it hit me; was it so obvious that I liked Shlok? Did I do something that showed Vishal? But I liked Shlok just normally, nothing romantically or sexually, but what if subconsciously I was doing something else?

"But why do I even have to think about it? Why is 'us'," I gestured at Shlok and myself, "even a question?"

"Yes, why dude?" Shlok interjected. I could not help but notice how he was listening to our banter with interest until now.

Vishal just shrugged.

We talked a bit more, laughed a lot more, and then Vishal dropped me home around three in the morning.

I walked in my dark bedroom and noticed how soundly my family was sleeping, and I realised that except for the two calls that I had made to Dhruv—first informing him that I am going to Shlok's for poker party, and then at 11PM telling him I would be late, Dhruv had not even bothered asking where I was or if I was fine. I know I have been taking care of myself since forever, I have never needed anyone's protection, not now, not growing up, but it is always good to know that someone cares. I am not saying that Dhruv does not care for me, deep down I know he does, and he loves me a lot, but it won't hurt him to show it once in a while.

And as I went to bed that night, a message popped on my phone from Shlok asking if I had reached home. A sting of hurt pierced the back of my eyes as I answered him *Yes*. Small gestures, no matter how old the relationship is, small gestures matter a lot, and so do big ones. And as I closed my eyes for the night, tears escaped them from the side as I realised how happy I had been in the past few hours, how Dhruv and I have not laughed this freely in so many years.... Well, I cannot say much about Dhruv as he does not share anything with me. But I do... I tell him everything, tell him what I want, what I desire, and yet I am so unsatisfied. And as my tears turned into soft sobs, I went to the guest room to sleep as I did not wish to wake my family up by crying bitterly, and in the darkness, loneliness and sadness I realised I would never be happy like this ever again. What I experienced today, it won't come to pass again. That this was my life, whatever be it!

14 NOTHING CHANGED, BUT SOMETHING DID!

"So, you had fun last night?" Dhruv asked when I woke up at midday. I could hear Shiv and Ojha playing and making a lot of noise outside.

"Yes, quite a lot. What did kids eat?" I asked as I turned in the bed. He was sitting in the bed, working on his laptop.

"Apple and cheese sandwiches," he informed.

I checked the clock hanging opposite to the bed and saw it was 12 in the afternoon.

"And you?" I asked, stepping out of the bed.

"Sandwich as well," he informed simply.

I nodded at him and stepped in the bathroom to freshen up.

When I came back, he did not even look at me. I scoffed quietly, but maybe not so quietly because it got his attention.

"Huh!" he asked politely.

I just shook my head and walked out, and my kids ran in my arms to wish me morning and demanding why I did not come home last night on time. I talked to them, discussed what I had been doing, and promised to spend the day playing with them. This had them settled and they retreated to the room where all their toys were kept… well, not all their toys because a lot of them made way to all other rooms and at present my house was nothing but a mass of littered toys and Lego pieces.

Entering the kitchen, I started prepping for lunch, while fixing myself a very quick snack to eat and calm my grumbling tummy.

"What did I do now," Dhruv sighed as he stood beside the sink and asked.

"What did you not do?" I demanded, avoiding his gaze.

"I am trying to figure out both," Dhruv muttered. "Mind being helpful here?" he teased. His tone was light and casual, like always. The best thing about Dhruv was, he was never angry!

"I had a great time last night," I informed.

"That's great! You should have fun," Dhruv was genuinely happy.

"But that is it, isn't it," I snapped. Somehow his happiness that I was happy at another man's house rose fury in me. "I would only be happy in other people's house and not in mine."

This rendered him quiet.

"I was happy, for the first time in God knows how long, and *that is great*?" I scathed. "Why am I not happy in this house?"

"What do you want?" his asked politely. "I would do anything to make you happy and you know it."

"I do not want shit!" I snapped again. "You bloody well know what I want, and you know it is not materialistic."

He blinked but he did not reply. Did he even understand that I wanted his time, attention, affection, love, passion….

I waited, but he did not reply. I turned away from him with anger boiling my veins and I directed that anger to tackle the dough I needed to do for the *chapatis*.

"You want to go out today?" Dhruv asked after a thought.

I stared at him and then shook my head. "No, but you take the kids to the play zone. Shiv wants to do bungee jumping, at least someone in this house should be happy!"

That day I spent time playing with my kids as I had promised them. We played UNO, badminton, chess and carrom, and by 8PM they were exhausted. I felt guilty, as usual, that I was not spending enough time with them. But it was a necessary evil and I only hoped that they would understand.

I forced dinner down their throats, and they were asleep by 9PM, which was surprising because they never slept before 9:30 even on school nights.

"Wow!" Dhruv spoke as he sat beside me and stared at my laptop. "New book?" he asked.

"Yes," I grimaced. I had just started writing a new chapter for my upcoming book, and talking was distracting me from the plot I had in my head.

"Which one?" he asked.

"What do you want, Dhruv?" I asked seriously. His sudden interest in my life was not fooling me!

"I just want to talk to you," and he caressed my hair but I slapped his hand away. "Shift," and he pushed me and flopped beside me in the bed and pulled me in his arms. I slumped. He wrapped his arm around my stomach, and I groaned. Not because I hated it, I would never hate his touch, but because his touch had stopped raising goosebumps all over my body and it was not a good thought.

He tried to nibble my ear, and that was it.

I pushed him and sat back up. As I looked down at his face, his handsome face that was torn with confusion, I sighed. But then, that sigh within me turned into anger because it was not my doing. I was not in the wrong, he was.

"For how long?" I demanded, seething with anger.

"What how long?" he asked, closing his eyes. And I knew he too was trying to compose himself. But I did not care.

"For how long you would pay attention to me and then leave me writhe in my misery, *again*?" I demanded. His eyes flicked open.

"What do you mean?" he asked.

"I mean, this time for how long you would show interest in me and my body, and then go back to ignoring me, so that, you know, I am prepared," I grunted. "Because, I am young, even if you are not, and having sex once in a couple of months takes a toll on my body and mental health!"

He did not say anything to this announcement. Yes, I was young and had sexual desires, but he was not that old too. I knew a few sixty-year-old men who had better sexual desires than my husband. But whatever the age maybe, he was once young too, he maybe almost forty-five now but he was thirty when we got married, and he had never shown me the desire that I have always housed in my body. And while the logical part of me told me that maybe he was gay, but I knew he was not, because at times, when he had shown interest in me, genuine love and interest, it was no way possible that he was gay! He was straight, or as straight as a man could be who is not at all intimately attached to his partner.

"You know I had a great time with Shlok last night," I barked, and his eyes closed again. The words in a normal context may hold entirely different meaning but Dhruv knew I was loyal to core… "We talked about so many things."

"He is your manager, it is his job to talk to you about issues," Dhruv sighed.

"Even personal issues?" I asked with raised eyebrows, "Is it also his job to make me laugh and smile. To ask me if I am okay? Like really okay? Or that he spent hours beside me, making sure I was not alone, even in my head?"

Silence met these words.

"I am lonely, Dhruv," I spoke as tears choked my throat.

"I am here," Dhruv muttered softly.

"But you are always busy on your phone or work. And if you are busy in neither, you are off doing something else or sleeping. You do not talk to me, you do not spend time with me, you do not even touch me. You are an incredible man, a wonderful father, but I have been telling you this for more than ten years, you are my husband, my partner, and not my father. I already have a father; please, treat me like your wife, and do not just ensure I am fed and physically well. I want a husband, Dhruv, not another father… but ever since we have been married, it seems like that's all you have been to me, another fatherly figure!"

Dhruv did not reply to this comment. How could he, or what could he say when I have been complaining about this for so long.

"Dinner?" Dhruv asked after a very long quiet moment, in which silent tears just dropped from my eyes. They were the tears of rejection, of the silent treatment I was so used to getting.

"I am not hungry," I muttered. I had prepared a full meal for us both, but I had no appetite for it now.

He slumped further down in the bed and stayed awake. He occasionally drifted off to sleep, I could hear his snores every so often, but he was forcing himself to stay awake.

"What can I do?" he asked around midnight.

"You can start by accepting that when you married me, you did not bring a little girl in your house to protect her. Yes, I was immature, stupid and whatnot back then, but even with those flaws, I am your wife. And you need to see it. You need to see me as your equal, as someone with whom you can share anything and everything, who deserves to know what goes in your head, because if you don't, Dhruv, one day I will stop talking to you, and that day would mark the end of this marriage."

I had opened up my mind, my heart to him, but he did not respond. He just lay beside me, and around 12:30 his snores filled the room. I got up and slid to the opposite side of the bed because I knew Shiv would fall off, the way he was fidgeting in his sleep.

And as I went to bed, though I was already in it for hours now, I knew nothing would change in my life. Because it was not the first time I had spoken these words to him and if he had not reacted before, why would he react now! But there was one thing that was different this time…. For the first time in fifteen years of meeting him, another man's face was flashing in front my eyes, another set of brown eyes were peering down my soul, trying to understand me. And I was craving to be in someone's arms, to hide away from my pain and loneliness, and for the first time those arms were not of my husband, but of another man's… a man who was, up until last night, absolute stranger, and while I still did not know a lot about him, I felt I knew him just enough to call him my own, even if, like a friend.

15 NON-FUCKING-NEGOTIABLY POSSIBLE!

Nothing changed post that declaration, well, maybe not nothing. Dhruv started paying a slight bit more attention to me…. A slight! He now started talking to me a little more, like maybe five-ten minutes a day and I could tell how much effort it took on his part to do that. And it was a far cry from what I wanted, what I truly needed in this relationship. I mean, seriously, can a five-ten minutes conversation take so much toll on someone? Am I so bad? Am I so hideous? Am I so horrible that my husband, my life partner cannot even talk to me! And this thought broke me even further, put me in worse mental state, if that were even possible.

I do not know what heinous crimes I had committed in my past lives that I deserved such husband and parents!

My parents, ruefully ignorant parents, had four children. Myra, my elder sister, is a year older than I am, then my brother, Rohan is ten years younger than me, and then Sohan was twelve years younger than me. Sohan passed away when he was two and it tore my family apart. I was fourteen years old back then and it was a loss I would never wish for even my worst enemies. The pain and suffering of losing a loved one is too much to bear. And it broke my parents. My parents, who always did ignore me, became even more distant than before. Myra and I have been the accidental kids, or so I have always thought of us since I understood *reasons* in life. My mother was a doctor, a struggling doctor, who prioritised her career over her children, and whatever maybe her reasons for it, it ruined us. My father, another struggling doctor, and a borderline drunk, had made us his punching bag. He had temper issues, like most men in his egotistical generation, and took it out on his wife and children.

So yeah, my life growing up was horrible. Myra was all I had for a decade, and we were growing up however best we were able to, but even between Myra and me, Myra was the dear one. As I am now a mother myself, I do not blame mom for it. I love Ojha a lot, more than my life, but the attachment I have for Shiv, my first born, I do not think I can ever develop for Ojha. And while I hate this thought whenever it blossoms in my head, I cannot ignore it. It was the truth. So yeah, I was the second child, and while youngest child is supposed to be most loved and adored, I was not. Well, my parents had no time for me!

And then a decade later, as I was getting some sanity in my life, my brother was born. And while it was my mother who bore him, Myra and I became his true moms. We practically raised Rohan. I still remember changing him at nights, feeding him from bottles, taking care of him, and making sure he was healthy and fine. And then two years down the line, Sohan came. And Myra and I became moms of two babies. I still remember dividing chores between us two. And splitting nights who would stay awake with Sohan. Yes, a pair of twelve-year-old and thirteen-year-old girls were raising two boys while their mother was raising her career.

I don't remember what I felt when I was little and taking care of my baby brothers, but I do remember often praying to God to give me fever so that my parents would check up on me, pay any sort of attention to me, show me any, maybe even tiny bit but any kind of affection! But I got none. Maybe I deserved none.

When I had taken Rohan in my arms for the first time, I still remember that day because I was in love with my brother from day one. And while my childhood was ripped off from me that day, I had not known that the little love that my parents ever shred on me would also be taken away because they only had as much to spare!

But what about my husband? Why did he not love me? Was I that unlovable? And with that thought I just continued with my life.

I did not set foot in the office for a long time, and while I did not speak to Shlok in person, I stayed in constant touch with him through other modes. We talked work on calls and mails, as it was required, but also on WhatsApp, where we stayed in touch on all the non-sense things. He was merely two years older than I was and I felt an incredible bond towards him. And the bond and friendliness between us grew so strong that it made Vishal once call me to ask where the hell Shlok was!

"How would I know where Shlok is?" I remarked when Vishal asked me the question.

"He is late for a meeting, he was supposed to meet me in office, and I cannot reach him," Vishal grunted.

I knew Shlok was going to office today, but that's all I knew.

"Okay, but why the hell I would know where he is?" I demanded this time.

"Because you always know where he is!" Vishal replied and it stunned me.

Was it the case? Truly?

"He never tells me a thing, but you always know where Shlok is."

"That is so not the case, Vishal, I am not his personal assistant," I snapped. Truly offended with the underlying meaning, if I was getting it right.

"Umm, you knew he went to Mumbai two weeks ago, while no one else did!" Vishal started, and it was the truth. Shlok had told me he was going to Mumbai, and like a stupid blubbering idiot, I had told it to Vishal when we were talking, but in my defence, I had not known that Shlok did not tell it to anyone else. "You know when he hits the gym," Vishal continued, and it was true too, I also always knew when Shlok did not go to gym, "and you always know when he is going to take a break!"

"It is because I talk to him," I interjected, "and unlike many other people, I try and talk about other things as well when I am talking about work. I feel it forms a bond. And Vishal, I am not his personal assistant, and I do not know where the hell he is at the moment!"

And I disconnected the call, feeling exceptionally irked. Was it true, did I only know where Shlok was at all times. I checked my WhatsApp, he was supposed to be in office at the moment, but he was not there. Should I ask him about it? But I just shook my head and went about my work. It was not my place to know where Shlok was, or whatever the fuck he ever decides to do with his time.

But if truth be told, my heart did flutter a bit at the thought of knowing that only I knew where he was. That he too felt comfortable with me. That he liked me, if not as much as I liked him—I still wake up to the sound of his laughter every morning—but I was glad that he liked me!

And as I went to gloomy, cold, horribly lonely bed that night, it hit me. I realised that the itch I was feeling all day to know where he was, to know what he was doing, and to make sure, to make quite sure that he was alright, told me everything. Because all my life, I have never felt like this for anyone! Men have asked me out, before marriage and after marriage; they have craved my attention all the time, no matter whether my husband was sitting beside me. But I have, never before, craved attention of any man! Not like this, not unless that man was my husband! So, all this means only one thing. Shlok was different. Shlok was something more. And unfortunately, quite unfortunately, I have fallen for him so hard, that it was unacceptable. And anything between us was absolutely, totally, non-fucking-negotiably possible.

16 QUESTION: WHAT DO I WANT?

The thought of having feelings for another man broke me to a new level. And this realisation did entirely something else to me. It made me wall up, brace myself as I was now ignoring the only good friend I had made in my recent years. But while I tried to ignore him, how do you truly ignore your manager?

I, at least, stopped talking about personal stuff with him, or as much as I could because keeping my mouth shut when talking to him was a mammoth task!

But the feelings were driving me crazy. As horribly alone I was in my life, talking to him, those few moments of exchanged smiles and laughter was my only solace. And I was depriving myself of those too, and it was horrible. Fucking horrible! But I did. I stayed away from him, even avoided talking work with him for whole ten days, and while I felt it eased the growing pains in my chest a bit, it did not fade.

And that's when I knew that it was not some mere infatuation I was housing for that man, my feelings were real. Too damn real… I was, almost certainly, falling for him. And it was not his fault… it was not his doing. He was kind and compassionate to everyone, I was nothing special. But to me, he was special, because while he was kind, caring and loving to everyone he met, I never met people who were kind to me!

I wonder why… maybe it was my *karma* or something that I only attracted pigs!

But it was true. So true that whenever I thought of him, I felt a physical pain in my chest because I missed him so much. And this forced another thought in my mind. My kids! What was I doing? Holy shit! What the fuck was I doing? My parents ruined my life, they forced me to grow up in an ugly environment, and was I paving the same path for my children too? An all too consuming guilt laced my heart and soul, and I felt I was drowning in the misery.

The thoughts and pains were growing so intense with each passing day that I did not know how to take it any longer. The guilt never faded. And as I was seeking help, desperately wondering what to do, God, yes, I believe in the invisible force, showed me the way.

Polar Technologies tied up with a counselling company, and the day when I was feeling so low that I was feeling suicidal—thoughts that were not alien to me as I have been suicidal almost all my years in Jaipur, thanks to my childhood—a mass email was sent from the counselling company asking people to enrol if they needed help! And I did… and help came.

I was diagnosed with something that I could not even remember the name of, but depression, panic attacks and borderline self-harm thoughts were very common in it. And so, I was given twice a week therapy with a certified therapist.

And the therapy began, and for the first time, I had someone to talk to, open to, who would listen and respond appropriately.

Tina was my therapist, and she was good, or as good as a first-timer like me would believe. She listened to me, consoled me because I broke down more times than I could count, and she helped me. She told me that having feelings for another man, while still being married to the greatest father of the century, was not wrong.

"Nyra," she spoke on the day when I opened up about my all too wrong feelings for Shlok and how it would affect my children's future, "if you remove the societal element, why are your feelings wrong? There is a raging gap in your life, a longing that craves to be filled. If Shlok is the person who fills that gap, then why is it wrong? It is not like your husband has!"

And her words hit home with me. If anything, my feelings were pure for Shlok, I genuinely liked him. I did not want anything from him, I just liked him for the happiness and smiles he gave me, and mind you, he gave me nothing else. So, why was I wrong? Why were my feelings wrong?

"But no matter what, I do not wish to ruin my kids' future, I do not wish to leave Dhruv," I sniffed.

"A sad mother is worse than a single mother, Nyra, always remember that," Tina had explained. "And while I am not allowed to talk to the spouses, I will make an exception, if you wish, I can talk to Dhruv and help you both!"

And she talked to Dhruv in the next session. She had assured me that she would honour the patient-doctor confidentiality code and would not pass on anything intricate to Dhruv, but she would just try and see what could be done to help me.

She talked to us together, she talked to us separately. She gave us homework to work on our relationship, and while Dhruv first took it in stride, listened to Tina, he soon fell behind. I could tell he wanted us to work, he wanted to do things to make me happy, to make this relationship happy, but he just could not do it. And after a while, Tina too gave up, well, on him, not on me! I wanted to change, for the best interests of my children, and I knew I would change.

So Tina worked with me, she gave me many tools to aid me, not physical tools, no, she gave me mental tools.

Techniques to help me take charge of my situation, techniques to help me overcome the hurdles that life throws at me, and I could happily tell that they were working. Helping my mental state.

But she did nothing to help me get rid of feelings that were brewing within me for Shlok.

"They are feelings, Nyra, I cannot do a thing to help you get rid of them," Tina had soothed.

"Can you not tell me something that helps me build a wall around me to avoid these conflicting feelings?" I had begged.

"Your feelings are not conflicted, you like this Shlok guy, and your feelings are genuine for him. They stem from the right place, from needs and desires that are awfully unsatiated, but they are not conflicted. What is conflicted is your mind, and you need to decide what you want; only then we can continue."

And we did not continue. Because I did not know what I wanted. And because I did not know what I wanted, Tina did not know how to help me!

"I am ending therapy," I informed Dhruv after six sessions with Tina.

"Why? Is it not helping?" Dhruv asked with a concern.

"No, I am ending it because I know it is not me who needs therapy, it's you! And it is not me who is the fucking problem in this relationship, it is you!"

Dead silence.

"You could not even do what she asked you to, isn't it?" I screeched.

"I tried, but–"

"But what?" I demanded. "You did not have the time? For me? For us? What the fuck is more important that this marriage to you?"

Dhruv just shook his head at this. "It was useless, anyway," he retorted, and I snorted. I snorted so loudly that

Ojha, who was sleeping peacefully in between us, stirred in her sleep. Dhruv patted her down to sleep again.

"You don't love me enough to even try, isn't it?" I asked, feeling so hurt that I felt my heart was about to burst out of my chest.

"Who said so?" he demanded this time.

"Then show it? Actions speak louder than words, but hey, you never say that you love me, you just don't say a fucking word!"

"Language, Nyra, what is wrong with you?" Dhruv complained.

"What is wrong with me?" I blanched. "What is wrong with you? Are you so fucking stone-hearted that your wife craves your love, and you cannot even provide it?"

"I do everything for you," he raged too. "I take care of children, I take care of this house, I rush around the city to pick up and drop off the kids… and you say I do not care for you?"

I was stunned by it. So stunned and shocked that a laugh escaped my lips.

"You take care of children, yes… but they are not just my children. You help around the house, yes, but this is not just my house. You rush around the city to pick up and drop the kids, yes, but again, hey, they are your children too… so why are you portraying that you are doing me a favour. Why the fuck is taking care of *your children* and *your home* a favour to your wife? Which sick century you and your parents are living in? What the fuck, Dhruv?"

He did not respond to this, so I added, steaming with anger now, "And how is taking care of children equivalent to taking care of me? Yes, you buy me things, but so what? It is our money, we both work hard to earn it, so you are not doing anything special! I also buy you shit load of things…. Yes, you make tea for me, so what? I cook food for you more times that you make me tea. Yes, you help me with some chores, but so what, I take care of all the other chores all by myself! So how on earth are you taking care of me? If you had genuinely taken care of me, you would have taken me on that vacation I have been dying to go on for the past three years, but hey, our last vacation was eight years ago, before Shiv was even born! If you cared for me, you would have made love to me like my body craves, but no, you don't even touch me! If you cared for me, you would have taken the therapy seriously and understood what I need to be happy, what *we* need to be happy, but no, you did not pay attention to Tina's words, you did not do a thing, Dhruv Manchanda, you did not do shit!"

And there was silence again. Dhruv stayed awake for a while, but then as usual, he drifted off to sleep. And tears pooled my eyes again. Why do I even try?

And as I went to bed that night, I thought about what Tina had asked me to. She had asked me to find out what I wanted in my life. Was it Dhruv or not. No, I did not wish to leave the father of my children, as ignorant Dhruv maybe towards me, he was an incredible father, and to be honest, the best one in the whole goddamn world. So, no, I don't want my children to be fatherless. But yes, I wanted Shlok in my life. But I did not know how? I did not want Shlok as my romantic partner but also not just as a friend, I wanted him more, so much more, but what was more—and that was the question, isn't it?

17 MORE... SO MUCH MORE...

Two more weeks passed, and nothing changed. But what changed was my dynamics with Shlok. I have been trying so damn hard to keep my distance from Shlok and it triggered him to ignore me fully. He only talked shop and nothing else, and while it hurt me horribly, I did not do anything to change it.

But as fate would have it, the Bangalore client came back, months after that meeting, and we finally won the deal. And this time they asked for Shlok and me to go down to Mumbai to meet them and sign the contract. I know Shlok could have gone alone, but he did not. He knew how hard I had worked for this deal to be signed, and he did not want to leave me behind. So, before I knew it, I was waiting for him at the Delhi airport on one of the not so cold mornings.

He was late, again, but this time I boarded the plane, and he came in just before the airhostess was about to close the gate.

I could not help but smile at him. He was panting, yes, but my face always breaks into a smile in his presence, and so it happened again.

"You are here," I beamed at him.

"I am here," he grinned too, as he shoved his laptop bag in the upper head cabin and smiled down at me.

"See you in Mumbai then?" I asked, unable to stop the rising feeling in my chest.

"See you in Mumbai then," and he jerked his head in my direction and walked away to sit somewhere behind me.

As he walked away, I felt a pang, a miserable jolt that told me I wanted nothing but to hold him and get him to sit beside me, to talk to him for hours on end and stare at his beautiful face, but of course he was not mine to stare, so I just stared ahead and braced myself to the unsettling feeling that always came with a plane take off.

We spent the day with the client, talking business and work, and it kept me healthily distracted, but not fully. Every time our bodies brushed, I felt an ache. And it did happen a lot because the room we were occupying in client's Mumbai office was too small for proper mobility. And while I did not feel sparks or any kind of rush of desires that were always shown in the movies, this occasional brushing of skin did put the pain in my chest into an overdrive.

But I endured, and around 4PM the contract was signed and we headed back to the airport. Luckily, this office was also very close to the airport, and we were in the airport by 5:30PM. But only to be shocked.

"Our flight is delayed," I groaned as I stared at the screen showing the time of flights.

Shlok went to the enquiry while I stood at a side; he came back and confirmed that yes, indeed our flight was delayed and now would take off at 10:30PM.

"Now what?" I asked.

"Now, we wait," and he led me out of the airport again and we sat at an open restaurant to wait out the time.

As we walked, I remembered something, "Hey, do you know today is my six-month anniversary in Polar Technologies," I smiled.

He looked surprised for a moment, but then he grinned and shook hands with me. "That is amazing, huh. Congratulations."

"Thank you…." I smiled, unable to shake the weird feeling—no, not the sparks or anything, but just a feeling.

"Guess you are lucky for this project then," and he smiled broadly. I did not know what to say to this, so I just shrugged and pulled out my phone and walked away to make a call.

I called Dhruv to inform of this development and knew kids won't be happy. And because the kids were in day care, I then called their teacher there and talked to them. Yep, they were not happy. And I spent good ten minutes apologising to my littles ones and promising them the world to ensure they were not too upset. After all, I had promised them that I would be home before they went to bed, i.e., 10PM, their bed time for a normal Friday.

Shlok waited patiently while I talked to Shiv and Ojha. And when I finally disconnected and dropped to my seat opposite him, he grinned.

"Kids, huh!" he remarked.

"Kids, yes," I nodded.

"I ordered coffee for you, cappuccino, hoping you like it," Shlok smiled again.

"I love cappuccino," I nodded, and looked at the menu.

"And ordered peri-peri fries," he added. "Assuming I could not go wrong with the fries."

But he did! But I did not reply. However, my feelings, like always, must have shown on my face because he spoke, "I did go wrong, didn't I?"

"It is fine," I smiled as I brushed my hand in the air.

The waiter arrived with our order and to show how okay I was with his choice, I picked up a spicy fry and popped it in my mouth, making it scream in agony.

"It is nice," I smiled, despite myself and gulped entire glass of water.

Shlok called the waiter and asked for plain salted fries as well.

"Never found anyone who does not like peri-peri fries," Shlok muttered as he took a shot from his incredibly small espresso cup, and I chuckled.

"Cute cup," I pointed, and he laughed too.

"Yeah, too small, isn't it?" he added.

"Yes, and I do not eat anything very spicy!" I sighed. "I used to, a lot, but I had a very complicated pregnancy with my son, and spicy food became a big no-no for me then. And then Shiv, my son, was hypersensitive to spices, he got massive acidity attacks if he ate even minor amount of spices, so I stopped putting chilly in everything."

"So, you don't eat chilly?" he asked seriously.

"Yes, I cannot eat chilly," I nodded.

He too nodded as he understood the background of the non-chilly rule and passed on the plate of plain salted fries in front of me that the waiter had just placed on our table.

"So, you are a tea or coffee person?" he asked after a pause.

"*Ghar ki chai, bahar ki coffee,*" I smiled again, and he nodded again. "I have a particular preference for tea, so only homemade tea for me, while I can have any kind of decent coffee," and I sipped my cappuccino. "What about you?"

"I like coffee more," he informed, and I made a mental note.

"Food?" he asked.

"I love South Indian, basically idly-dosa," I informed.

"I saw a South Indian café around here, we can go there," he added.

"I am fine here," I smiled, chewing the fries. "How about you?"

"I like non-veg, but you are a vegetarian, so you won't know what I like in particular," he informed.

"Yeah, that's true," I mused, "You can say any name and I won't understand it one bit."

And he laughed. His laugh was so light and casual that I felt a jolt in the pits of my stomach. It was just like the one I heard each morning in my sleep, yes, six months have passed and yet, I still wake up to his laugh each morning!

"Girlfriends?" I asked as I sipped my coffee.

"None as of now," he shook his head, "had a few in the past, but none that lasted for long."

"Why? None suitable to be married?" I asked, curious.

"Can say so," he grinned.

"I got married when I was 22," I spoke, and he blinked at this.

"Wow, that's too early," he spoke, once his shock had subsided. And I just shrugged.

"I too almost got married when I was 22 or 23. My back then girlfriend wanted to get married, and we were engaged and all too, but then, we did not!"

"Dodged the ball, you did," I nodded solemnly.

"Yeah, thinking back, I do believe I did," he smiled.

"Yeah, but I did not dodge the ball," I groaned.

"Yeah, you did not," he spoke in a sad tone. "But you have two incredible children."

"I have," I smiled at the mention of my children, and we talked a bit about Shiv and Ojha. He was a good listener, he talked and discussed a lot about my kids and about the children of his friends and family.

Later he left to use the washroom and I dropped my head on the table and sat in the quiet. He came back after a while and asked, "So where were we?"

I groaned and lifted my head. My hand, that was stretched all towards his side, was mere inches away from him. I withdrew it, fixed my shirt, and wondered how it would have felt if he, by any chance, had taken my hand and squeezed it. No one has ever held my hand in an affectionate sort of way, neither my parents, nor my husband, so, I could not help but longingly stare at his long, thin fingers and imagine how they would feel wrapped around mine.

"Have you heard this song?" he suddenly spoke as he pointed in the air, bringing me out of my miserable thoughts. And only then I noticed the song that was playing in the background, but I did not recognize it. I just shook my head.

And he started singing it.

"*If you hear something late at night, some kind of trouble, some kind of fight, just don't ask me what it was… just don't ask me what it was…*" And I stared at him in amazement. He sounded so happy when he sang….

"It is Luca, by Suzanne Vega," he mentioned the song as I smiled at him.

"Never heard of it," I shook my head.

"It is a very nice song," he informed, and I quickly searched for it on my phone and added it to my song library to listen to it later!

"So, what made you start writing?" he asked.

"De-stress," I smiled. "Writing puts my head in right place," I informed.

And he raised his eyebrows. He was about to say something when his phone started to ring. He just checked who was calling, then put it on silent.

"So, you should write more often, Nyra," he encouraged.

"I do write, though these days I do not find the time," I smiled.

"Then find time," he insisted, and his phone rang again.

"You can take this call, you know," I spoke as I pointed at the phone he had just put on silent again.

"I am talking to you, and I more of 'in the moment' kind of person," he announced, and it happened. His words raised such a volley of emotions within me that I could not express. He was talking to me so he had put his phone on mute and put it upside down so that it could keep on ringing, and he won't be bothered.

We talked for a bit more, then he paid for our coffees and fries, and we walked inside to board the plane.

"Try to sleep this time," he muttered as we boarded the plane, he helped me stow away my bag in the upper head cabin and left for his seat.

And as I buckled my seat and closed my eyes— my whole body was aching and tired and this seat was the closest to a bed I could get at this instant—I realised how much his words meant to me. No one, literally no one had ever put their life, even a second of it, on hold for me, and this guy spent uninterrupted four hours in my company and not once did he look at his phone. As tears escaped my eyes, tears that I knew would never dry up because never again in my life will I have another day like this, I knew that this was the moment I would never forget. And much in future, in days to come, when I would reflect on my life, I am sure I would realise that it was this day, that moment, when I had first fallen in love with Shlok Rajput, the man who was supposed to be just my manager, but had turned out to be much, so much more.

18 TIME TO SALVAGE THE MARRIAGE!

Now with the contract signed, we kicked off the project. Shlok asked to split the team in two. One team to work from Bangalore office to cater to client directly and visit them regularly–supervised by Misha, and another team in Delhi to cater to all the technical work–supervised by me. And we began the work. The team I got was new and less experienced, and it just caused a wave of issues. Day after day some or the other technical issue popped up, and night after night I debugged and ensured the project was going on smoothly.

While the intention of setting up team in Delhi was to work with them on the ground, the work and long hours did not allow any room to visit the office. It also hardly left any room for any interaction with Shlok, which I did not mind, or so I said to myself to control my feelings because I missed him. I often reminisced over the day we spent together in Mumbai. But two months passed in a haze of firefighting, and in early March, we delivered the first part of the project—POC, i.e. Proof of Concept, and I went to Bangalore to deliver the POC in person. Shlok did not accompany me this time.

The client was delighted with the POC and they signed up for a bigger and better project, with much higher value.

And we celebrated.

Shlok threw a party for all the project people in Delhi and asked Misha to take out Bangalore folks to some nice restaurant. It was the first time I ever went to a bar, and I was stunned. I don't drink because I have very low tolerance to alcohol and I really never truly enjoyed it. So, I had never gone to a bar before, and now, with two small children, it was out of the question. So, colour me amazed when we went to the best pub in Delhi. I started off with a Virgin Mojito and moved up to varied coloured punches. A lot of my team members took assortment of drinks, and Shlok drank whiskey.

"You don't drink?" he asked me as he eyed my glass.

"Not in front of people," I smiled.

"What's the worst that could happen?" he asked, laughing.

And my mind said, 'I can confess my feelings for you for the entire team to hear,' but my mouth said, "I can do something utterly stupid and live to regret it later."

And he laughed again, so wildly that a part of me felt he was drunk but he was not.

Everyone was just sitting, drinking, talking and eating, and I was bored. Why was there no life in here! I wondered. The live music in the pub was amazing, and I could not help but feel my body sway with the music.

"Anyone up for a dance?" I asked the group in general.

No one responded but just stared at me as if I had grown horns on my head.

"Wow! You all are a dud crowd," I complained.

Shlok raised his eyebrows at me, so I asked, "Why? You also don't dance!"

He, obviously, missed the 'also' in my statement, because I was comparing him to Dhruv, who does not dance, like at all! Well, not with me at least.

"I do dance," he spoke with furrowed brows.

"Then dance with me," I challenged.

"A little later," he shrugged.

I pouted and sat back wondering how good my bed would feel instead of this hard chair on which my bums were currently placed.

Around 10PM, four of our group left. I too stood up and wondered how on earth would I go back home at this hour when Shlok asked, "How do you plan to go back?"

"I am wondering the same thing," and I turned to the other guys in the group to ask where they were heading, to which Shlok said, "Let me know when you figure it out."

And I wondered if he would be chivalrous enough to offer to drop me home? And that made me realise, with a jolt, Dhruv had not asked me how or with whom I would come back home. He knew it was not safe to travel alone post 6PM in Delhi; he knew I was frantic about it. He knew I always took precautions as I have been groped multiple times in my growing up years. Yes, boys in the city, or maybe in the neighbourhood I had grown up in, were awful! But my husband did not ask me, did not bother checking up on me. He did not offer to pick me up! I mean I have been taking care of my safety since the beginning, even when I was a little girl I had to protect myself because my parents were never around, and if I told them who did what, they blamed me! But even now… what did a girl need to do to get little bit of attention from her husband? From the man who loved her….

"Okay?" Shlok asked, apparently, he was waiting for an answer from me.

"What?" I asked, now way too upset to even remember what he had said. My sad realisation had turned my upbeat grin down.

"You would tell me how you plan to go home, right?"

I nodded grimly. He looked at me with a puzzled look, then commented, "And I thought we were going to dance," and just like that he stood up and started shaking his body.

Following his lead, I stood up too and started to dance, and the rest of the group joined us as well. We danced for a while, and in those moments, I had so much fun that I did not wish for the night to end. Then, one by one, people started to drift off, and I found a team member who actually lived quite close to my place. I shook hands with all present, waved goodbye to Shlok and left, feeling a bit of unease in my chest. Because while the immense work and long hours, and no constant chat with Shlok was keeping my feelings at bay, it was not a permanent solution. And with the time we spent together, laughing and chatting in the pub, it felt like a hole had been ripped open in my chest. And as I sat in the car, getting closer to my home, my family, I could not help but feel sad and alone. And this made me wonder about another thing, how fucked my life was that I would feel alone in a house where I actually lived with my husband and two children. This is so not done. And to make the matters worse, a message popped up on my screen from Shlok saying, *Message me when you reach home.*

I sent him a thumbs up as acknowledgement and stayed quiet during the entire car ride. The team member driving me home was also not very keen on talking as I felt he may have had a little too many drinks and was driving with epic concentration, so I did not distract him. I liked it this way, it gave my heavy heart a lot of time to unload whatever shit it was holding in!

Work resumed the coming week and it became brutal. The expanded project came with some serious technical issues. Earlier I had a team of eight members, but now, thirty-three people reported to me, and I was drowning.

Shlok started getting involved as he tried to help. Well, it took a lot of incessant whining and complaining from my part for a month for him to start devoting his precious attention to my project, but in the end, I got it. And while professionally it was a huge help, he was taking some load off my plate, personally, it wreaked havoc.

Now, I talked to him at least four times a day, and it resulted in me talking about him nonstop at home too. Soon my kids knew his name and often asked me when would 'Shlok uncle' come and visit them. I don't know if Dhruv noticed anything but the fact that I could not help but smile whenever I took Shlok's name must not have escaped his inattentive eyes. Because, for starters, and for very mysterious reasons, he had suddenly started showing interest in me. He was more active, a little bit more communicative and hell, he even tried to woe me in bed at nights. And while all was good, for once, I felt my body cold to his touch. I have been feeling cold to his touch for a long time now, courtesy of getting rejected uncountable times in bed, but I guess it was the guilt that I now housed for having feelings for Shlok that made me feel even worse.

So, I again tried to create distance from Shlok. And deep down I think it pissed him off rather brutally this time because he started lashing out at me, though not very strongly but quite subtly. But I knew what he was doing, he could not say upfront that my hot and cold attitude was bugging him, so he was saying it this way. But I could not dial it down, even a notch, because I was growing fond of this man at an accelerating pace, and the last thing I wanted to do was fall for him to the point of no retreat.

And one night, as I felt Dhruv nibble my ears and caress my stomach to get ready for some physical activity, Shlok's face flashed in front of my eyes. And while I responded to Dhruv equivalently—my husband deserved a devoted, loyal wife, not some cheating, raging bitch—I made a resolve to do something about it. And as we went to bed that night, all happy and satisfied, I zeroed in on the best thing I could do to salvage this marriage; I decided to resign!

19 STUCK OUT OF BED!

My resignation email was ready. I had written it over and over again, curated it for days, and now all I had to do was send it. But I did not! I just could not. Partly because my project, the one I had worked so hard on, was still on-going. And while the entire project was to be done in a year and a half, I dreaded to imagine living a life I have at present for another year or so. And partly because I did not wish to leave Shlok, even if we had a weird ass relationship! So the best reason for delaying, that I could think of was, I would at least see the Phase 1 done, which was due in another two and a half months. I owed this much to Shlok. My notice period was two months. So I waited for another two weeks and then I turned in my resignation.

And the moment I had hit sent, I counted till twenty, and my phone started ringing; it was Shlok. And even without hearing his voice, I could tell he was pissed.

I picked up the call, and even before I could say 'Hi', he said, "I will see you in office in thirty minutes." And he disconnected.

"But there is huge rain prediction today," Dhruv spoke agitatedly when I dressed up to step out. Yep, it was raining in March, global warming was at its peak now! "Doesn't make sense to leave now," he added with a concern.

"I don't know, I will be back as soon as I am done," I assured.

"But it is already post lunch, why do you have to go now!" he stressed.

"I sent that resignation email and Shlok wants to talk in person."

Dhruv did not respond to this; he understood corporate world just as well as I did. So he just nodded and spoke, "Stay safe, okay."

"I will be, and it is not raining yet, maybe the prediction is wrong," I winked and headed out as the cab I had called had just gained entry in our society.

An hour later, I was sitting in a closed cabin in front of Shlok, who looked epically grim. He had just made some small talk with me when I had arrived in the office, and then had chivvied me to this cabin.

"So," he started as he exhaled.

"Yes," I nodded.

"Why?" he asked.

And I just shrugged.

"I need a reason," he insisted.

"My reasons are personal," I replied honestly. "I mean the workload is insurmountable, yes, but my reasons today are personal."

"I will ease up your workload," he fired up. "I have anyway decided to hire a scrum master for your project, I will move Swati right away to your account to support you. It should make your life easy."

I knew Swati was a good scrum master, she was managing Vishal's project until now, so if Shlok was giving me Swati, he was for sure pissing off Vishal.

"And what about Vishal?" I demanded with raised eyebrows.

"Swati will manage two projects, anyways with you and Vishal leading the projects, a full-time scrum master does not make much sense," he stressed. I considered him for a moment, and while I did not agree with him fully, I just shrugged. I have been leading my project for a while now, and I had sneaked a peak in Vishal's project when I had helped him debug it, and in both the projects, I knew, we needed a full-time scrum master. But well, who was I to comment.

"But that's not the main reason for my leaving," I added grimly. He looked so stressed, with his expressions torn, it seemed he was in pain, like in actual physical pain. And it did something to my heart that I could not explain. "Shlok, I cannot explain it, but I need to leave this organization!"

"Why?" he asked in a gruff voice.

"Because I have to," I shrugged, trying to put up a smile on my face. And while my smiles always came involuntarily in his presence, I noticed how hard it was to smile today.

"I need a reason and you can leave," he muttered, rubbing his face to gain some composure.

"Why do you want me to stay?" I asked in a barely audible whisper.

And he let out a harsh laugh.

"You will find someone to replace me, I know it," I muttered as I recounted in my head that I would lose my marriage by staying in this job. And while Shlok can replace me, I cannot replace my husband!

"I would, would I?" he was so sarcastic that I flinched. He had never been sarcastic with me, angry–yes, on edge–yes, but never like this.

"I will put in my resignation in the system. With two months' notice, I will be able to deliver the Phase 1, and you will have enough time to find my replacement," I patted my thighs in agitation and started to get up, but he lifted his finger to indicate that he was not done yet.

"I need a reason," he asked again.

"They are personal," I shrugged again.

"But I still need them," he insisted. "If I have to go through finding a replacement of you, to find someone like you again, I think I deserve a better answer than 'personal'."

"I don't think it is prudent of me to tell you," I spoke, and he laughed. He actually laughed and repeated the word 'prudent'. Of course, it was not prudent. How could I tell him that hello, I want to resign because I am falling in love with you, or hell, maybe I have already fallen in love with you!

"Do you have another job yet?" he asked sincerely.

"I don't, but it does not mean I won't find one in two months," I shrugged.

"Why don't you resign when you actually have a job in hand," he suggested.

"And you would let me go, without any hard feelings?" I asked with raised eyebrows.

"I can never have hard feelings for you," he sighed, and my heart skipped a few beats. "This is your personal decision, and while I would like to know what is driving this decision, I cannot force you to stay."

"Shlok," I whispered, and I almost spoke the words I wanted to say… but I didn't. Instead, I turned on my phone and put it in selfie mode. "Pic? I forgot to take one in Mumbai."

And he stared at the screen, his left eye was twitching as I clicked the pic. I wonder what he was thinking at that moment. But instead, I asked, "What's wrong with your eye?"

"Nothing," he rubbed his eye.

"Are you camera-shy?" I asked seriously.

"No, I am not camera-shy, Nyra," he muttered. "Have you thought this through?" he asked grimly. "About resigning?" he added as I looked at him quizzically.

"I even made a pros and cons list," I nodded and patted at the notebook that was placed in front of me.

"What is it?" he demanded and without any invitation, he picked it up and flipped it open.

I had made the list only last night, and it read—

Pros:
Better work life balance
Better health
More time with the kids
More time with Dhruv
Manageable working hours– considering I would start writing again

Cons:
Lack of salary (meh!)
WMH

Shlok's eyebrows went up so high that it almost disappeared. "It is a 'meh!' to you that you would lack salary?" he asked.

"Money is of no importance to me, I am not a very materialistic person. What I want or desire can easily be managed with the money I earn from writing. So yeah, meh!"

He looked stunned by this answer.

"Money does not matter to you?" he asked again.

"I never had any money to play around, Shlok, my desires, my needs, my wants are non-materialistic. I am happy and content with the basic necessities," I shrugged.

"What do you mean? I thought your parents were doctors," he asked, shocked. "Why did you never have any money?"

"Long story," I sighed.

"And you want non-materialistic things, like?" he encouraged.

And Dhruv's laughing face flashed in front of my eyes. His attention, his affection. And my heart fell. The intimacy he had started to show a few weeks ago, the one that had made me resign, had died down again. Yes, I firmly decided to resign two weeks ago, even though it was again three weeks since he had even touched me, or hell, lay beside me! I don't know what I was chasing in my marriage, but love, intimacy and affection were not somethings that were in the horizon!

"Love," I whispered. "Time..." I added solemnly. "Attention!"

Ringing silence met these words and then he asked the final question, "What is 'WMH'?"

"The only thing that makes my heart drop to the pits of my stomach whenever I think of leaving this place," I muttered mysteriously.

"And that is?" he asked enthusiastically. "Good to know there is something that makes you excited about working here," he added.

"It is personal, Shlok," I sighed.

"Tell me," he insisted. "You have to tell me if you want me let you go without holding any grudges."

I considered him for a moment and then took back my notebook.

"I will take you up on your offer and won't resign unless I get a better offer from somewhere else," I nodded. "And I will tell you the truth of my leaving then, but not today."

I do not know why I changed my mind. Maybe I never really wanted to resign because the thought of leaving him, even if he wasn't mine to keep, was killing me. Or maybe, I had decided to leave because I did not want Shlok's face to flash in front of my eyes every time Dhruv kissed me, but well, Dhruv was not kissing me anymore, he anyway hardly kissed me, hardly paid any attention to me. Yes, Dhruv cared for me a lot, but again, not like a husband. So, if he was not going to kiss me, why should I feel guilty of Shlok's face flashing in front of my eyes.

"What is WMH?" Shlok asked again.

"I will tell you one day, but that day, we cannot be in office, in public place or somewhere we can be overheard," I asked.

"So many conditions," he laughed, but his laughter was restrained.

"So many damn conditions, yes," I nodded.

"But you will leave," he asked.

"I was never here to stay," I sighed, "and I do not have any intention to be working in a corporate for a long term. I just do it to pass my time, to be independent. My passion lies in writing and one day, I will pursue it."

He did not reply to this resolve and opened the door to the cabin. But as we stepped out to the office floor, I realised it was empty. Eerily, empty. And it was quiet! So damn quiet, well, except for the pounding of the rain, that was pouring heavily. As we walked up to the window, I realised the entire compound outside was flooded.

"Holy fuck!" I cursed. "How long were we in the cabin?" I demanded and I opened my phone to check the time.

It was 7PM, and I knew that night, I was stuck in the office and was not going to get into my bed.

NO, DON'T GO THERE! 20

Shlok walked around frantically to check for others. But there was no one there, except for the security guard at the main door, and he was shocked to see us. Apparently, everyone was shepherded out half an hour ago when there was a warning of major water logging issued by the authorities.

While Shlok called everyone from admin to security head, I called Dhruv to inform him of the latest developments.

"I am stuck in office," I cried.

"I have been trying to reach you for an hour," Dhruv sounded angry. "Your phone was unreachable."

"I was in a meeting room, maybe network was an issue there," I sighed. "And Dhruv," I paused.

"Yes," he asked, panicking now.

"While I was in meeting with Shlok, the entire office emptied. No one is here; only the security guard is here and no one else!"

"What?" he bellowed. "They left and did not bother checking all of the meeting rooms? What kind of admin does your company has?"

And I wondered the same.

"Are you okay?" Dhruv asked in mild panic.

"I am fine," I assured him. "Are kids home?"

"Yes, I picked them like two hours ago, when it started to drizzle. I thought it is better to keep them home in such weather, where I would have liked for you to be too." And I could hear his frustration in his voice.

"I will come home as soon as I am able to," I assured him.

"Stay in touch and conserve phone's battery. Power may go out so please, please, be careful," he insisted.

"Yes, I am not alone, thankfully," I groaned.

"Yes, stay with Shlok, and don't get hurt okay," Dhruv spoke in the same insisting tone.

"I will, you too also take care and of the kids," I spoke and then we disconnected.

I turned and found Shlok staring at his screen a few feet away from me.

"What do we do now?" I asked Shlok seriously.

"Wait it out," he spoke as he pointed at the window, where it was pouring like hell.

"And why did no one inform us that they were clearing out the office?" I demanded.

"I asked the same. Apparently, they forgot to check the only room we were sitting in," he grunted. "But good thing they did not, because I talked to four different people, and they all are stuck in the worst traffic jam ever. Two of them are thinking of getting out of their cars and swimming their way back to office," he sighed.

"Well, in this weather, what else can be expected?" I muttered as I went ahead and took a seat. I pulled out a novel from my bag and flipped it open to read it. I was in no mood to work now. Yep! I always carried a novel in my bag, just in case I find some time to read.

Shlok too slumped in a seat beside me and asked, "What should we do about dinner?"

I closed the book and sighed. I wanted to talk to him, hell, I wanted to talk to him every second of every god damn day, but I feared that if I started talking to him, if I let myself open up to him, I won't be able to stop. And then the hole in my heart would be blown-up to epic proportions and then it would be very difficult to manage it.

"I don't know," I shrugged. "Maybe something from the pantry… or downstairs cafeteria, whatever is edible."

And he walked away to find us some sustenance. I did not know what to do. Honestly, I would do anything to keep my distance from him, but well, have you looked at this guy! Can you blame me for feeling a desire to be closer to him. He is so generous, caring, affectionate and kind. He is also so handsome and ambitious. Why, hello, he was the youngest president in the organization, and I don't think that he gained that position by doing the dirty tricks. He was so damn hardworking and driven that he got that position. So yeah, in a nutshell, that man was a full package of my doom.

He came back with his hands full of biscuits and chips. And he dropped them in front of me. I raised my eyebrows at the contents on my desk.

"For dinner," he smiled as he picked up a packet of chips and started munching. Soon the packet was empty, which he threw in the dustbin and closed his eyes and sat in silence.

As my eyes fell on the dustbin, I pulled one out from under the desk, turned it over and placed my aching legs over it. Then I turned to my book and started reading it. But could not concentrate. Was he really sleeping? Or was he just resting? Does he snore like Dhruv? Or was he a light sleeper like I was? So many questions were churning in my mind when he asked, "Is the book any good?"

"It is…" I trailed off, "… fine."

"So, bad?" he asked with a smirk.

"Actually, it is good, it is a bestseller, but I do not see what the fuss is all about. It is way too predictable. I mean I could tell who the killer is just after a few pages," I shrugged.

"I have read it," he spoke as he opened his eyes and smiled, "I could not!"

"Really? You could not tell that the therapist himself was the murderer?" I asked in shock. I was on the final pages of the book and the big showdown was very disappointing.

"I actually could not," he pondered, "how did you guess?"

And I thought about it; I just knew that he was the murderer.

"I don't know, I just knew it. Maybe because I am a writer and I think from that perspective," I thought out loud. "You know, how would I pivot the story, how I would mould the characters, you know what I mean."

"I don't know what you mean," he laughed, "but I understand."

I nodded.

"So?" he asked a bit awkwardly.

"So what?" I asked seriously.

"Tell me something no one knows in this whole company," he pointed around to show the office.

"You already know about my writing," I smiled.

"And I am sure Vishal knows it too," he grinned. And when I stared at him, he said, "I told him. I was just so proud to know that my team member is a national bestselling author that I just...." And he waved his hand to show how he blabbed.

I felt humiliated. I pushed my face in my hands and spoke, "It was a secret. I do not want people to read what I write knowing I wrote it."

"People love what you write, I have not read your books, but I have read some reviews, why are you even ashamed?" His expressions said he could not believe it.

"I don't know, people I know always say I write very cheesy romance," I made a face. "But..."

"But what?" he asked intrigued.

"But I write from my heart. A romance that I crave, I desire, and because it comes from my heart, it is so good that people fall in love with my stories," and I felt tears sting the back of my eyes.

"Your husband must be one hell of a lucky man," he laughed.

And the tears fell.

"Hey," he was instantly beside me. "What's wrong?" he asked, pulling my chair a bit towards him, concern written all over his face.

"I write good romance because that is my fantasy, my desires. And because my desires have no outlet, I pour them out on paper," I sniffed.

"What do you mean?" he was stunned.

"I mean," I sniffed to control my emotions, "while my husband is an epic man, the best in this whole god damn world, the best father… he… well, let's just say, he is not a romantic or even a talker. I am the vocal one in the house, while he, he does not say a word to me, does not talk to me, and neither does he express himself nor does he acknowledge my feelings."

And Shlok was quiet, dead quiet.

"But you love him," he asked seriously.

"Yes, very much so," I spoke so quickly and confidently that he was stunned. "He is my best friend, Shlok. Before we got married, we were best friends. And it does not matter to me if he does not love me like I want him to, but I love him just enough to do anything to keep this marriage going."

Shlok did not say much after that. After another hour or so, we went to the security guard to ask for some dinner from downstairs cafeteria, and the guard came back with two plates of food, after finishing his own meal downstairs.

Then, Shlok showed me a small room where there was a small bed put in for medical emergencies and practically forced me into it.

"What about you?" I asked seriously.

"Don't mind me," he muttered as he closed the door shut. And I just stared at the door. His sudden mood change was very much off putting but I did not know what to say. His laughing, cheery self was all but gone, and in its place was a brooding man.

And as I went to this teeny tiny bed, I wondered what did I do wrong. He was not this upset even when I had resigned. Yes, he was upset, but he was not so closed up. But he was now, and I could not help but notice he shut down when I confidently said that I loved Dhruv, that I would do anything to make my marriage work. So, does it mean what I think it means? No, no, I would not go there. I would not let myself go there, because if I went there, there was no coming back. And for the sake of my children, I would not go there… I would not do anything to break my family.

LEARN SOME CONTROL! 21

I was barely sleeping, the sound of the rain had dialled down a lot but the sound of my heart thudding did not let me have any moment of peace.

I had messaged Dhruv that I had eaten and was now going to sleep in the small medical room of the office, and he was relieved. While he never showed me how much he loved me, he always cared for me, no matter what. And it showed today more than ever.

The kids were upset, as usual, that I was not home when they went to bed. Afterall, it was I who always tucked them in the bed each night and read them a story. But Dhruv did manage well whenever I was away and so he did today.

At around 2AM, a soft knock on the door made me sit upright.

I jumped out of the small bed and opened the door and saw Shlok there.

"You want to take the bed?" I offered very quickly.

He just shook his head and spoke, "The rain has stopped and the roads seem clear on GPS; want to leave now?"

"Leave for?" I asked, but I picked up my phone, nonetheless.

"My place," he said, and I just stopped dead.

"Your place?" I asked with raised eyebrows.

"It is closer and not waterlogged, if it is okay with you," he added.

"I trust you," I whispered so softly that I did not know if he even heard it. Well, I did trust him. And I knew he had two beds in his home, so I could take the spare one.

"So, let's go," he smiled in relief and walked away.

The drive to his house was a quiet one. The traffic was not there but there was a lot of water logging and he drove very carefully. Last thing we needed was to get stuck in some ditch or water hole! But by the time we reached his house, the rain started pouring even more heavily. Thankfully he had underground parking, so we were not wet.

We went upstairs, and he offered me clean pair of clothes to wear and a towel to dry myself.

"My pajama would be a bit loose for you," he muttered, "but you can tie it up," he suggested.

I nodded and retreated to the bathroom of the spare bedroom. When I stepped out of the bathroom, I found a pair of slippers and a quilt on the bed that I was supposed to use for the night. Shlok must also be in the bathroom because I could not hear him anywhere.

I went to the kitchen and checked the fridge. It had milk, so I poured some in a pan with some water and started to make some coffee. I remembered he liked coffee and not tea.

"Coffee?" I spoke as he came out and offered him a steaming cup.

"Coffee at 3 in the morning?" he asked as he wiggled his eyebrows, but took the cup nonetheless.

"With the day we have had today, I felt 3AM coffee is called for," I grinned.

And he gestured me to sit on the sofa. I sat beside him, but then soon, I put my feet up and almost lay down on it, pushing a cushion under my head.

"I am so tired," I groaned.

"I can imagine it," and he too just sat with his eyes closed, sipping his coffee.

"Nyra," he muttered.

"Shlok," I sighed, and I feared it came out as such a raspy breath that it sounded almost inviting.

From the corner of my eye I saw his eyes flick open, and I closed mine shut to save myself the embarrassment.

"You never answered me," he spoke after a pause.

"About what?" I asked, still eyes closed.

"Something that no one in the office knows," he muttered.

"I want to lose weight, but I am unable to," I groaned.

And he laughed.

"Why is that a secret? Everyone wants to shed some kilos but is unable to," and he laughed again.

"My weight is something else," I muttered.

"What is your weight?" he asked seriously.

I finally opened my eyes and looked at his face, he was staring intently at me.

"More than a decade ago, I had a neurological disorder," I sighed, and his brows furrowed, "my neural system is very weak. I almost lost my legs in the process."

"What?" he blanched.

"Yes, dad saved me. I was in hospital for six months. The ability to walk is something we take for granted, but when I lost it suddenly, it just broke me, it was a very hard phase of my life, and even harder for me to get back on my feet. When I had walked into that hospital, I was 54 kilos, I got severe medication, and in two weeks of those injections, I was 74 kilos," I grimaced.

And his face hardened.

"The drugs they gave to save my nervous system did something to my body, and I am 70+ ever since. Within weeks, I went from size M to XXL," I sighed.

"But you are able to walk," he summarized.

"Yes, with a fucked up hormonal system and weight imbalance, but yes, I can walk," I smiled. "And as my family says, that is a trade-off they can live with."

"They are absolutely right," he nodded.

"Yes, but it was the hardest time of my life, that moment when I was diagnosed, and the fear that it had entailed that I could never walk?" I sighed.

"I cannot even imagine," he sighed too.

"But I survived," I nodded. "Despite everything, I survived."

"You were married back then?" he asked seriously.

"Yes, imagine shit like this happening in the very first year of the marriage, hell, even before you get to celebrate the six month's anniversary," I snorted.

"Seriously?" he was shocked.

"Oh yes, Dhruv was understanding. He loves me, he was incredibly worried for me. But his parents," and I grimaced.

"Let me guess, they were not happy?" he mock laughed.

"Duh! They accused my parents of hiding my illness, saying why else something like that would happen so soon after our marriage. They actually accused us of just dumping my sorry ass in their son's lap to get rid of me," I laughed, and Shlok looked horrified.

"But Dhruv had known me for two years by then, and he knew it was a random occurrence and not something I was hiding. He tried to explain to his parents, but his parents just dismissed him. Told him that he was hiding it all for my sake, because I had him wrapped around my little finger, turned him into my personal lap dog."

"They did not," Shlok looked outraged.

"Oh, they did. And you know what was the worst of it all?" I asked, as I rolled my eyes.

"I don't think I want to hear it more," Shlok hissed. "But do tell," he sighed.

"They forced me to have children. They did not care in the world that I was mere 22 years old, that my legs were still on the mend, that I had a nervous system that could practically break with any minor impact, and they practically pestered me to have children," I laughed.

"But why?" Shlok could not believe it.

"Because," and I exhaled heavily, "they thought I was going to die or end up bedridden. And considering Dhruv was madly in love with me, losing me to any illness would break him, and then they would not have any grandchildren. So, they wanted me to have at least one boy child… mind you, not any child, but a boy child, before I died."

And silence met these words.

"But you waited," Shlok asked seriously.

"Yes, six years. Till we were sure my body could support a baby in me… and then we had Shiv. And then Ojha," I smiled.

"Shiv and Ojha?" Shlok asked.

"Shivaya and Ojaswi, Shiv and Ojha for short," I smiled again at my children's name.

"Beautiful names," he smiled back.

"I know," I beamed.

"So, that's my history," I finished.

"And you are struggling with your weight ever since?" he asked seriously.

"Yes, and considering I now literally eat my emotions. You know I was not that big on eating before, but I have been keeping things in me for so long, now I am an emotional eater. Anything may happen to me or around me, even minor, and I have to stuff my face, and if I won't eat, all hell will break loose," I grimaced.

"That is very bad, you need to see someone for this," he suggested.

"Meh! I think I need to stay happy to avoid it," I smiled.

"Then why do you not stay happy?" he asked so seriously that I blinked.

"Happiness is relative, Shlok," I sighed.

"And what does that mean?" he asked suspiciously.

"Never mind, now, tell me something about you," I asked, propping my head on my hands to face him.

He thought for a moment, then spoke, "My dad passed away when I was ten, mom raised me along with my sister. It was a very difficult time for us all, especially mom. But mom remarried when I was around fifteen. And ever since my mom remarried, she is better and happier," he smiled at the mention of his happy mother. And I beamed at him. I understood what he meant. While my mother had off loaded pile of her shit on me when I was growing up, deep down I never wanted her upset. Like they say, mother is always a mother, no matter how good or bad she has been.

"That's amazing," I spoke as I smiled up at him. And he smiled back.

"What else?" I insisted.

"What else?" he thought for a while, and then said, "I have travelled around the world. I have so far visited seventy-two countries," he grinned.

"Wow!" my mouth hung open, "I mean, wow!"

"Yeah," he grinned.

"Which one was your favourite, and don't say America!" I laughed.

"Actually no, my favourite was Turkey," he spoke after a thought. "It is amazing. And next would be Brussels, Belgium. Actually, Brussels was my first international trip, so I guess, that would always be special for me."

I just stared at him as he reminisced about the fond memories of his travels, and I felt so happy in the moment. I actually felt so complete that I really did not wish to go to sleep. But I had to, it was way past 4 in the morning now, and I had to go back home tomorrow morning, so….

"Bed?" I asked, getting up from the sofa.

He looked a bit shocked, but then nodded. And turning off the lights, we went to our respective rooms, and I closed the door shut. I stayed glued to the door for a long moment, wondering. I had never imagined I would land in Shlok's house in the middle of the night, and most definitely I had not imagined landing in his spare bed. While I had no sexual fantasies towards this man, I did have some feelings. Feelings that strengthened at the thought that he did not even attempt to flirt or lay a finger on me even when I was alone in his house, and no one knew I was here! He was such a gentleman.

I walked to my bed and noticed that the AC was already turned on, he must have done so for my benefit as it was way too humid today! I felt myself melting at this gesture. And then I realised that I was missing a water bottle. I walked out and saw his bedroom door was open. I peered inside and saw him lying on the bed, AC's cold air drifting outside and the lights from his dressing room streaming into the room.

"Is this how you sleep?" I asked, puzzled.

"Yes, how do you sleep?" he enquired, lifting his head to look at me.

"In pitch dark," I laughed.

"Okay," he nodded and closed his eyes again.

Unintentionally, I felt my legs drift a bit towards his room. His bed, half empty bed looked so inviting that all I wanted to do was lie beside him and sleep in his arms.

"Okay, good night, Nyra," he spoke in a firm voice.

And suddenly I realised what the fuck I was doing. I was lingering at his door in the middle of the night, like a stalker! And he had to dismiss me… shit!

"Good night, Shlok," and I backed out slowly.

And as I went to bed that night, feeling stupid and embarrassed, I realised how big a fool I was to do what I just did. And while I had feelings for him, such strong feelings for him, he had none for me, and that was great. Because if he did have those feelings, there was in no way I would be able to control myself.

22 WELL, A GIRL CAN DREAM!

I woke up around 10 in the morning the next day and panicked that I was not home. Then I remembered where I was, but I was supposed to be with my children. I called Dhruv from bed and informed him that I was in Shlok's spare bedroom.

He was relieved to know that because most of the Delhi was submerged in knee deep water and while he had tried to find a route to come to office to pick me up, he was unable to find one.

"Is it?" I blanched as I walked up to the balcony to look outside, and true enough, from the height of seven floors, where Shlok's apartment was located, I could see water everywhere. I looked down at the gardens of the society and saw kids playing in water. The society apparently was much above the road level and the society at least was not flooding.

"What do I do?" I asked, panicking.

"Stay there, I do not want you to be stuck in rains and flood, okay," Dhruv ordered.

"Are kids okay?" I asked. "And what about food for them?"

"Neha offered to cook for them," Dhruv informed. Neha was our downstairs neighbour, and her son was Shiv's good friend. And we often traded favours as both Neha and I were working women and supported each other.

"Oh, thank God," I sighed.

"Or I would have cooked for them," Dhruv spoke indignantly.

"Yes, your famous *poori sabji*," I mocked. Dhruv was an excellent cook, but he could never cook *chapatis*. So, whenever he did cook, he made *pooris* as you can never go wrong with deep frying anything.

"Yes," and he beamed with pride.

"Tell kids I will see them soon," I requested, and he agreed. I deliberately did not talk to them as I did not wish to upset them. Ojha, for sure, would have started crying on hearing my voice. And then we disconnected.

Firing up the Uber app and putting in the drop location, I went to freshen up. And when I came back, my jaw dropped. The fare that came up was three fucking thousand! And the time shown was seven hours… the roads must be horribly clogged, because I lived almost two hours away from here in normal traffic!

Sighing, I stepped out of the room, but could not find Shlok anywhere. I could hear music coming out of the third room which had been locked before, so I knocked on the door.

The music stopped and he stepped out.

"Your hidey hole in there?" I mocked.

"Umm," sheepishly he opened the door and my jaw dropped. It was a gaming room, with a massive TV and a PlayStation hooked to it. "I do not allow anyone in here, and keep it locked when I have visitors."

"Okay!" I spoke as I scanned the collection of games that lined the wall along with so many photographs from his life. The wall opposite to it had a bookshelf with at least two dozen books. The photographs intrigued me, so I looked at them all, walking at a slow pace along them, trying to find Shlok in each of them and noticing how he had changed over the years. He, honestly, looked funny in his younger age, and

I wondered if I would have liked him back then? The answer in my head was instant, if he was the same person back then, the same kind, passionate, funny, and hardworking person back then, then yes, I would have liked him.

"So, what are you playing?" I asked him seriously.

"Well," and he turned on the TV and a football game was on pause there.

I raised my eyebrows at him, and then picked up a book from his shelf and plopped myself on a seat in the room.

"You can play, while I read…" I smiled. "And I am sorry, you would have to endure my company a little longer, the roads are clogged, and I cannot go home yet!"

His face split into a grin at this, making me wonder if he wanted me here?

"You can stay as long as you like," he smiled.

"As long as the rain god likes," I replied with a smirk.

"Hungry?" he asked and as if on cue, my stomach grumbled.

"What can we eat?" I asked and he left for the kitchen, me on his heels.

"I have eggs," he pointed.

"I can make omelettes," I nodded. I was a vegetarian but I loved omelettes mainly because one of my uncles cooked them for us when we were little at his home and we developed a taste for them!

"But I don't have bread," he sighed. "And I want bread with my omelette."

"Do you not have a shop downstairs?" I asked.

"I do, but it is raining," he pointed out of the window.

"So what?" and I pulled out a five hundred rupee note from my wallet and put on my slippers. "I will go and get you some bread, the least I could do," I smiled as I walked out of the apartment.

"You don't have to," he complained as he picked up the keys and followed me.

"Oh, come on, it is lovely weather outside," I laughed as we stepped in the elevator and stepped out at the ground floor.

"Are you sure of this?" he asked as he stared out in the rain.

"Well," I smiled as I squeezed his arm, "if kids can have fun, why can't we?" and folding the money in my fist tightly, I ran out, with him on my heels.

We raced to the shop, and by the time we reached there, we were absolutely soaked. Thankfully I was wearing a dark coloured shirt else everything would be visible from within. But still, I crossed my arms over my chest and handed him the money to pay for the bread.

Securing the change in the plastic bag that now also held the bread, we walked out, now much slowly.

We were heading to the building, when I said, "Hey, we are already wet, aren't we?"

"We are, yes," he spoke.

"Then," and I ran towards the garden, where there was a big puddle of water and splashed the water on him with my feet. He was stunned by my action. And soon, he was running after me to seek his revenge. We played in the rain for a while, where we splashed each other with mud, rain and whatnot, and then, when I started to sneeze, he led me upstairs.

My teeth were chattering by the time we stepped foot in the elevator.

"You are something else," he laughed as he turned off the fan of the elevator.

"You don't know half of me," I murmured, and he laughed again muttering something in the lines of 'crazy for sure.'

Back in his home, he rushed inside to bring out two large towels, and while he put one around his shoulders, he placed second one around mine and rubbed my arms to bring me some warmth.

And as he rubbed my arms, our eyes met, and I felt the sparks. He was so close to me that I felt his breath graze my face, and the way his thumb brushed against the side of my neck, my breath faltered. His eyes were now lingering on my face, and there was so much warmth in his eyes that I felt my knees wobble.

"Nyra," he spoke hoarsely. His thumb now was circling softly on my cheek, and I could feel my heart beat rapidly.

"I should go and take a shower," I spoke as I came back to my senses. This was not right, so not right… and while this was the best physical touch I have ever gotten in my entire existence, the most intimate I had felt with anyone, I could not let it go on. I just cannot.

Sighing, Shlok dropped his hand and pulled back. I rushed inside the room and locked myself in the bathroom to stand in a very cold shower—I forgot to turn on the water heater in the bathroom before!

Sneezing even more violently now, I stepped out of the bathroom, with a towel around my torso and noticed something epically shitty. I had no clothes. No underwear, no bra and no clothes. I rummaged through the wardrobe that was in the room and found some of his winter clothes, and that too just upper wear. And I stared at them painfully. Shit! I went back to the bathroom and quickly washed my undergarments for later. I knew they won't dry in this weather, so I'll maybe ask for his iron to dry them, or maybe wear the wet ones, if presented with no other option.

I quickly put on a hoodie I found in the wardrobe, and it dropped till my mid-thigh. Okay, that's the best we can do, but the thought that I had nothing underneath this hoody made me epically conscious.

I lifted my arms, and yes, my ass was visible, so I wrapped the towel around my waist to secure my naked bottom. And I dared and stepped out. But he was not there. Phew!

I knocked on his bedroom door, no answer. I turned the knob and the door opened. I could hear the shower running in the bathroom. Should I walk inside? What if he comes out of the bathroom completely naked? My eyes widened at the thought but still, better I see him naked then he sees me! Isn't it? And I raced inside and headed to his wardrobe, hoping, seriously hoping to find some shorts or pajamas to wear.

I was still shuffling through his closet, making a mess of already messed up piles of clothes, when the door to the bathroom opened and froze.

I knew he was standing at the door as I could feel his shocked gaze at the back of my neck, so slowly, very slowly I turned. I did not even know when both my hands had reached my teeth, and I was biting at least six fingernails in one go.

My eyes found his to start with. His hair was wet and tousled, and his eyes were fixated on me. And then my eyes trailed down his body, his chest was bare, water droplets still dripping from his chest hair, his black tits perked up, his chest muscles shifting with each breath he took and the perfect V of his waist ending in a towel. He was not flat or muscular like shown in the movies, but he was not fat either. He had some tummy fat, which did not look bad. Well, who was I to complain, I myself had a big flab covering my stomach, and Dhruv had an almost eight-month pregnant type belly!

My eyes lingered at his waistline and I could not help but feel my mouth water and a slickness spread up my thighs. Holy fucking shit! I was aroused. And as if this was the wake up call I needed, I looked at his face and found him staring at me with amusement.

"Umm…" I started. "I need clothes."

Understanding dawned upon him as he too registered what I was wearing.

"Sorry," I added hastily. "But I have no clothes!"

He nodded and walked up to me. I quickly stumbled backwards and fell on his office chair, which rolled to the farthest corner. He stared at me in shock, but when I steadied myself, he held back a smirk and turned to pull out some clothes for me.

"This works?" he asked as he handed me a t-shirt. I was ogling at his back muscles when he turned and noticed me staring. My face burnt as I realised that he knew what I was doing.

I took it without meeting his gaze, but it was too light for my curves. I really did not want to display my now very much perked up tits to him.

"Anything else possible?" I asked sheepishly.

He then pulled out another one. It was light too.

Why could he not give me any normal t-shirt. I know my father and husband wore t-shirts that were made of thicker material. Why did he have to wear almost see through ones?

"Any other?" I asked, feeling embarrassed.

He pulled out the entire pile and placed it on the table beside me and gestured for me to choose from it.

I quickly shuffled through them. None was fine.

I grimaced. Maybe I could wear four shirts to hide my curves! I thought sadly.

"What is the problem with my shirts?" he demanded.

"They are—" I started but then paused. "I—" I did not know how to frame the sentence.

"What?" he asked, feeling agitated now.

"Well, I need something that is of thicker material, you know," and I crossed my arms around my chest, hoping he would get my drift.

His gaze lingered at my chest for a moment, and then he did get my drift. He gave me an 'oh, I got it' kind of expression, went to another closet and brought back a formal t-shirt, just like I was hoping to find.

I nodded my thanks, and then waited. When he did not move to find me some bottoms, I said, "Pajamas, shorts, anything perhaps?"

And he slapped his forehead and offered me three options, with varied lengths. I chose the knee length pajamas and walked away to my room with a muttered thanks.

I changed and came back to find a packet of takeout food on the dining table.

"I ordered food from the restaurant that is in the society," Shlok informed me as he put the food in two plates. "I was surprised to see it was open when we went downstairs."

I nodded and took the plate from him and started to eat quietly.

"What do you want to do post eating?" he asked seriously.

I was so embarrassed that I could not even meet his eyes. So, I just thought about yawning, and a yawn came! "I feel too tired, maybe I will go to sleep."

He nodded, whisked away the plate as soon as I was done eating, and went to his gaming room. I knew I had upset him, offended him, but I did not know what to do! How could I be around him, when!

And as I went to bed in broad daylight, too tired and stressed, and yet not at all sleepy, I wondered what the hell just happened today. I saw Shlok almost naked… and I drooled over him… and I got aroused by him. Never, never ever in my life I have felt this sensation bubbling within me, so why now? And as I put in my audiobook to help me drift off to sleep, a very waking dream popped up in my head. A dream where I had bridged the gap with Shlok, while we both were wrapped in towel, and I had, very deliberately, raked my hand through his tantalizing chest hair while I pressed my lips firmly to his. And slowly, had let the towel drop!

23 A NEED TO MISS HIM!

I stayed in bed for a few hours, where I kept on checking the GPS and various cab apps to see if I could go back home. I did not know what to do here!

It was around 4PM when he knocked on my door.

"Come in," I sighed as I sat back up. He opened the door and the way the light from the corridor was highlighting his body and his beautiful face, he was a sight to behold.

"Are you not hungry?" he asked, and I saw he was carrying quite a few packets of snacks. He dropped them on my lap and went to sit on the other side of the bed. He picked up one packet, opened it and offered me to eat. And considering I was hungry now, I obeyed.

"This is awkward," I muttered. "I never thought I would ever feel awkward with you!"

"Then don't feel awkward," he replied a bit uneasily.

"Same to you," I spoke, and I could not help but laugh.

"But why is it awkward now?" he mused as he sat on the bed comfortably, stretching his legs out, and plopping himself on a big pillow.

"I don't know," I spoke. Well, I did know, because I wanted to kiss him, and it was not right, so not right. But I do wonder why he was feeling awkward.

"Okay, then let's talk about something else," he smiled. "What personality are you?"

I did not even know what that question was! So, I answered, "A very weird one!"

And he laughed, so loudly that I could not help but smile with him. "That I agree to," and laughed again. "But are you an introvert or an extrovert?"

"I know you are an extrovert," I commented, and he gave me a 'duh! Obviously,' kind of look. "What do you think I am?"

"I think you too are also an extrovert," he spoke after a thought.

"Actually, I am an introvert," I informed.

And he looked so shocked, that I added, "Over the course of years, I have learnt to adapt. To mingle, to make small talk, but all that drains my energy. And while with practice I can talk to people easily now, I find it tiresome."

"I cannot believe it," he was shocked. "I mean I have seen you talk to so many people in office alone!"

"Because I have to, I know I cannot survive or grow in a corporate if I don't mingle, right? Learnt it the hard way in the past," I just shrugged.

"True that, but seriously, you pull it off quite awesomely," he grinned again.

"Thank you," I bowed humbly.

"So, this," and he pointed between me and him, "is it also because you have to?"

"You are my manager, of course, I have to talk to you," I rolled my eyes, "but no, I do not get bored or feel drained when talking to you."

And the spark that flashed in his eyes in the moment said more than I wanted to hear. And it was too much!

And we were back to feeling awkward again… damn!

"So, personality?" I spoke after a pause.

"Oh, yes, there is this test, about 16 personalities, and it tells who is what, have you taken that test?" he asked.

I just shook my head, so he added, "Want to take it?"

"Sure, why not?" I spoke and he sent me the link on my phone. I opened it and started answering.

"Wow! That's a long survey," I laughed after filling half of it.

"I know!" he laughed with me, and I noticed that he too was filling it on his phone.

"Done," I commented. I got INFJ-T personality meaning the 'Introverted, Intuitive, Feeling, and Judging personality'.

"I am also done, and hey I am still the same," and he showed me his phone, he got ENFP-T personality, meaning, 'Extraverted, Intuitive, Feeling, and Prospecting personality'.

And as his eyes fell on my personality type, his expressions changed.

"What?" I asked, surprised.

"INFJ are quite rare, you are the first one with this personality that I have found," he smiled.

"Really?" I asked. "Well, I am one in a million kind of person," I winked, and he laughed.

"Let us see your compatibility," and he searched for something and showed it to me on his phone. It was a 16 X 16 grid with various personalities listed and who was the most suitable for whom. And while green colour signified 'It's got a good chance', blue showed 'Ideal match'. And surprise-surprise, INFJ and ENFP were a blue match.

"Wow! Our personalities are ideal match," I spoke hoarsely.

"True that," he whispered.

And it was awkward again. Fuck!

At around 6, the skies cleared, finally, and I got the call from Dhruv saying he will come down to pick me up. But as tempting as that offer was, I did not want my kids to be stuck in this dirty weather, in a car! What if the car broke down in some waterlogged area, what would Dhruv do then. So, I shot him down and checked the apps which I had been monitoring. Now the distance between my house and Shlok's house was less than three hours.

"Better than six hours, hey!" I chimed as I stepped out of the bed, to change my clothes. As I turned to look at him, there was such a vulnerable look on his face that I did not know what to say.

"I need to go, Shlok," I whispered. "My children are waiting for me!"

And as if he came out of some trance, he nodded and stepped out of the room saying, "I will let you change then."

I had never thought it would come to this, that I would fall for a guy who was not my husband. I mean, I have never been in such a situation before! I never had unrequited feelings for anyone in my life. I had a boyfriend in college, bloody bastard cheated on me, may he rot in hell, but even he liked me back. And then I met Dhruv, and well, our story is not the normal kind, but he loves me truly. And now there is Shlok. I don't know what he wants from me, what he needs from me, but I just want him. Not in any dirty, sexual manner; I think if I ever showed my palm to any astrologist, he/she would say that the sex-line is not even present on my palm... no, I want Shlok as my friend, as my best friend, as a friend with whom I can spend hours... and maybe, maybe, sometimes I can kiss him, touch him.

'Oh, shut up, Nyra,' I scolded myself as I put on my clothes, thanks to occasional ironing during the day, my undergarments were dry now.

I put his room and his bathroom back in order. And putting all the clothes I had worn during the day in the washing machine, I booked a cab.

"The cab is ten minutes away," I announced as I placed my laptop bag next to the entrance.

And it was awkward again. While we waited, while I kept on checking the app for progress, it kept on getting more and more awkward. Shit! What was it? And why do I feel that he wants to say something.

The cab was just two lanes down, maybe I could wait downstairs, I thought.

Yes, I should wait downstairs, and firming my resolve, I finally looked at him. He was standing a few feet away, leaning against a wall, looking at his phone. But why did it feel like he was not actually looking at his phone, but was waiting on me?

"I will go now," I muttered.

He looked up, surprised. Did he really forget I was there?

"Oh, sure. Cab's here?" he asked.

"Almost," I nodded. "Thanks for having me...."

"Thanks for being here," he nodded too. And I did not know what to make of it.

And I was almost at the door when something so powerful overwhelmed me that I could not feel my knees. I had to, I just had to.

So, I turned, walked back to him, and kissed him on his cheek.

Fuck! I did not just do that, the sane part of my mind barked. And the sane part was right because Shlok had absolutely frozen at my action. I know I should not have done that, but I just could not *not* do it! I had been dying to kiss his stubbly cheek for months now....

Heaving a huge sigh, I pulled back, only to realise he was holding my waist by his one hand and his second was on my arm.

"Why?" he asked as he swallowed the lump in his throat.

"I like you, though it is wrong, I just do," I sighed again.

"And what do you think I feel for you?" he spoke in such hoarse tone, my eyes widened.

"I do not know, and I don't think I want to know," I spoke, now meeting his eyes.

He was so close to me, I could feel his minty fresh breath on my face.

"Why?" he whispered as his hand, that was on my arm, trailed down to my fingers. He grabbed my fingers and I looked at them. A warmth, such tender warmth filled my chest at his small gesture that it took all of my self-control to not melt in his arms. No one ever held hands with me, no one ever showed me this simple gesture, that in itself feels so complete.

"Because, you and I can never become 'we', *ap aur main, kabhi 'hum' nahi ban sakte,"* I whispered, and his hand dropped.

"Is this why you resigned?" he asked, taking a step back. "Is it the not so prudent thing?"

"WMH," I spoke as I walked to the door. "Would Miss Him. Shlok, I am in this organization because of you. And the only con in the list that sinks my heart every time I think of leaving is *you.*"

And as his eyes widened in shock, I stepped out and closed the door behind me.

I finally reached home at 9:30PM, and the smiles of my children at my arrival was precious. I could tell they missed me, but Dhruv had taken good care of them. Of course, he did, he was the best father in the world.

But as I went to bed that night, I could not stop the feel of burn on my lips where they had touched Shlok's cheek. I could not help but feel his hand on my waist or his fingers around my own. And I knew deep down, no matter what happens, I was incredibly in love with that man. And that brought me to another resolve, no matter how much I loved him, he can never replace the father of my children… so now whether I stay in this job or quit it, I would stay so far away from him that I would always miss him. Hell! I need to miss him to keep my family whole.

24 THE DOWNFALL OF MY ENTIRE BEING!

Shlok did not approach me, he did not even message me, and even though it should not have, because I pushed him away, it pissed me off! Anyway, I kept on doing my work and he did not interfere. We interacted quite a few times a week, but it was always with wider team, and there, we acted perfectly normal. But there was a gentleness now when he talked to me, or maybe I was imagining it, but a soothing caress when he addressed me. I hope it was just my imagination because I did not want other team members to know or guess about something that was not there!

But I missed him... more than I could have imagined. Despite all my attempts to keep my distance, every morning, the first name I searched for on our Teams chat or WhatsApp was his. Every night, without fail, he starred in my dreams. If I found something, came across something I wanted to share, his name was the first that always popped into my head—well, along with Dhruv's, of course. I often wondered what he was thinking, if he missed me as I missed him. But I was almost in love with him; he wasn't in love with me, so why would he miss me? Did he ever remember the time we spent together, the talks we had? He might forget those little talks, little things, but I never would. I anyway never forgot a thing in my life. So, there was no chance I would forget my discussions and talks with him. They were the most precious memories for me, and I would cherish them all my life.

So far I have been to office six times, twice I met Shlok in office, and other four times I met other team members. And today happened to be the seventh time when I was going, mainly because my team called me as there were some critical things to be discussed, so of course, I had to be there!

So, after a month of kissing him, even if on his cheek, I saw him. He was standing far away, talking to someone else… another girl, as usual. And while it should not have bothered me, it did when he raked his hand through his hair and laughed the way he just did. I gritted my teeth and moved to sit on my desk when his eyes met mine.

And he paused. Even from this distance I could see a tenderness on his face when his eyes fell on me. I had not told him I was coming to office, but maybe team did because I knew he never visited office without any reason. Or maybe I was just overthinking it. Of course, I was not that important to him, but then why could I feel the catch in his breath when he noticed me. And it made all the difference. Until that rain incidence, yes, I will call it the 'rain incidence' and not the 'kiss incidence' even in my head, Shlok and I had weekly one-on-ones. But now, ever since that day, all that had stopped. Mostly because I dreaded to talk to him personally. I dreaded to face him, because I was scared of what would happen. What was he feeling? What was he thinking?

I closed my eyes and flopped in the chair, and two of my team members grouped around me to chat. I could not be more thankful to them. We talked, discussed so many things. I even had a few one-on-ones with them to address their concerns, but one can never completely avoid the inevitable.

And post lunch, it happened.

"Awkward?" he asked in a soft whisper as he sat on my desk, quite close to me.

"Will you make it?" I asked with a smile. Damn it! I could not help but beam when he was around.

"You tell me, you are the one who is avoiding me," he spoke very quietly.

"Nah, I don't think there is anything to avoid," I shook my head and he laughed. Fuck it man, I love that laugh. How I could hear it every damn day of my life.

"What?" he asked, confused. "And before you say nothing, you were staring at me quite weirdly."

"I was just thinking that you have a nice laugh," I replied without a second thought and crap! "I made it awkward again, didn't I?" I teased him, trying to break the sudden tension that had crept up on his face.

"You always know what to say, isn't it," he sighed. "Anyway, it is good to see you," he replied as he started to walk away, but I could not help it. He was so close to me after such a long time. How could I not stop him? But how could I stop him?

"How have you been?" I asked in a vain attempt to stop him, to stay closer to him, to breathe in his indulging perfume.

"I think just like you have been, feelings are mutual, aren't they?" and with a slight nod, he left.

Fuck it! Fuck it! Just fuck it!

His last words were still singing in my head, I mean seriously, feelings were mutual, really? I had an incredible crush on him, maybe one that was bordering on love; but did he feel the same way?

I was on my way from the washroom when I felt an arm around my shoulders. It was Roshesh. Another colleague of mine, though from a different department. But he was a good friend of Vishal, so I had talked to him quite a few times before.

"What's up?" he asked with a grin.

I turned and replied, "I am fine, how are you? Momma's boy?" I deliberately added 'Momma's boy' slang. He was often teased so, not because he actually was a momma's boy, but because of the old hit show, 'Sarabhai vs Sarabhai'.

He grinned again. Everyone, including Vishal, always said he was harmless, but I never felt so. Yes, Roshesh was very polite and friendly, but I always thought that he donned a mask, and he was so good at it that only a few times, very few times had I seen the truth in his otherwise always smiling eyes. And today, I don't know why, his eyes were reflecting something even more sinister.

"I heard you got stuck with him last month," he gestured towards Shlok, and I felt uneasy.

How the heck did he know about it?

"I was stuck in rain!" I replied simply.

"So, did you guys do anything?" he asked. And it was such a simple question, but the way he said it, the way his eyes moved and the way his face split in a grin, I knew what the hell he meant.

"We talked," I spoke with sour expressions.

"Oh, come on, Nyra. You know what I mean!" and he gave that pathetic grin again.

I exhaled loudly and said, "Not that it is your concern but no. I am married Roshesh, and I love my husband."

"So what? Married, loving people have affairs," he shrugged.

"Not me!" I spoke in disbelief.

"Good, I was hoping you were not one of his—you know…." and he trailed off.

"One of his what?" I snapped.

"He has a lot of girls on his all sides, hope you know that," Roshesh informed, and while I had heard many rumours about Shlok's affairs with office girls, I did not believe them. And anyway, it was none of my concern. "So, I am just warning you, be wary of him, okay?" he continued.

I pressed my lips into a thin line and nodded.

"Now that I have done you a favour, I need a favour," he spoke.

"Okay," I spoke.

"Promise to do it?" he requested, and his smiling self was back again.

"Depends on what you ask," I replied. This man, apart from a few interactions, was practically a stranger to me. How could he even ask that?

"It is actually quite a simple thing," he spoke in such sweet tone that I knew it was anything but simple.

"Okay," I spoke, now partly confused, partly scared.

"Sign this," and he pulled a paper from his back pocket.

"What is this?" I asked, shocked. Of course, I was not in any important position in this organization that my sign would matter anywhere... so, what was he asking of me, and why?

He placed the paper on the table, offered me a pen, and smiled, "Just sign, for me, please."

I looked at the paper. The words on it were hidden as the paper was still folded, and all I could read was the words *'Yours Sincerely, Nyra Manchanda'*.

"Unfold the paper, Roshesh," I ordered.

"You won't sign?" he asked, crestfallen. "It is not like I am asking for your money or property."

"But what am I even signing?" I demanded.

"Never mind," he shook his head, picked up the paper and started to walk away. But now I was too curious. As he moved to put the paper in his back pocket, I snatched it and opened it.

He tried to take it away, but I was horrified as I read through a few words. You could see it on my face; I raised my hand in front of me to stop him from coming closer. "Don't you dare," I hissed. "What the fuck is this?" I demanded.

He chewed his tongue but did not reply.

"You better tell me what the fuck is this or I am going to the HR," I warned.

"Revenge," he hissed.

"Revenge? This is revenge?" I fanned the paper in his face and asked again, "This is revenge?"

"He stopped my promotion, Nyra," he barked. "Any idea how hard I have been working? How many long hours I have put in? And he stopped my promotion. He is younger than I am… and yet he is a bloody President, and I am only an associate director."

I could tell Roshesh was older than Shlok, but still.

"So?" I raged. "So, he did not let you get promoted, so you will do this?"

"He deserves it," he grunted.

"No one deserves this," I said angrily. All this while I was trying to keep my volume low, but it was getting difficult by the second. "And he is not even your manager. You are in a different team. How did he even stop your promotion?"

"You do not know how people are promoted here, do you?" he laughed, and I just shook my head. "There is a panel of judges who decide the fate of people. And Shlok was on my panel. I had thought that all these years of chatting, gossiping would pay up for me, but no! The vote must be unanimous, and Shlok denied my promotion. Only he did! Imagine it. He did it last year too, bloody bastard!"

"So you would do this? You would ruin someone's entire life for a promotion, and the way you are behaving, I sincerely doubt you even deserve it," and I raised the paper again, "and you are going to use me? ME?" and I almost shrieked the last word.

Vishal was beside me now.

"What happened, Nyra?" Vishal asked kindly.

"Let us go in a cabin and talk," Roshesh spoke.

"I won't go anywhere with you, that too alone. So just stay the fuck away from me," I hissed.

Vishal stiffened at these words.

"What's wrong?" Shlok's voice also came from my other side. I was trembling with rage now. And while Vishal placed his hand on my arm to ask what was wrong, Shlok placed a light hand on my waist. "Nyra, are you okay?"

"Oh, now I see," Roshesh mocked as his eyes fell on Shlok's hand on my waist.

"Shut the fuck up, you bastard," I spoke so venomously that both Shlok and Vishal stared at me horror-struck.

"What happened?" Vishal demanded. "And what is this?" and he took the paper from my hand. He read through it and his eyes widened in horror.

"Nyra, what is this?" Vishal asked, thunder struck.

"I did not write it; he did on my behalf, and wanted to trick me into signing it," I almost shouted.

Shlok made to take the paper, but Vishal did not let him.

"Sir, it is not for you," Vishal shook his head.

"What?" Shlok looked confused.

"You talk to her, calm her down, I will talk to Roshesh," Vishal spoke politely. I was relieved that at least Vishal did not let Shlok read what was written on that page! It would have been devastating.

"I want it," I demanded Vishal.

"It will not land in anyone's hands, trust me," Vishal assured me seriously.

"It has my name on it," I hissed.

"And it will be burnt, okay?" Vishal spoke as he grabbed Roshesh's hand to drag him out when I almost screeched, "Hey, Roshesh," and he turned. "If you pull a stunt like this ever again, I swear I will tell everyone what kind of perverted low life you truly are!"

And as Vishal gestured at me to calm down, Shlok grabbed my arm and dragged me to a cabin.

"What was that?" Shlok demanded.

"What is it with you? How many girls have you screwed in this company? What is wrong with you?" I asked angrily.

He looked outraged, but not as much as I felt.

"How does it matter to you?" he asked as he crossed his arms.

And it was too much, I rushed up to him, grabbed his collar and shook him with all my might. "Do you have any idea what he planned to do? What he wanted me to do? How he was going to use me? Just because you have a playboy reputation?"

My eyes were filled with tears now.

"What was he doing? What was on that paper?" Shlok asked, but his expressions were not as outraged as before, they were soft. He grabbed my hands with one, and with second, he caressed my face.

I closed my eyes at his touch and felt a calm rush all over me. I pressed my face even more against his palm as tears now fell without any constraints.

"Let's go," he whispered. "We have a camera here, let's go."

"I don't want to go anywhere with you, Shlok, I just want to go home now," I sniffed.

"Don't be stubborn," he insisted as he dragged me out. My eyes must have been red and blotchy because when I reached my seat to pick up my laptop and my bag, my entire team was staring at me. They all tried to approach me to ask what was wrong, but Shlok just shook his head at them.

"Let's go, Nyra, we need to talk," he spoke firmly as he grabbed my elbow and literally dragged me out.

"Are you okay?" one of my team members asked seriously.

"I am fine, he is just dropping me home," I nodded.

And while they did not look convinced, they just nodded too. "I will call you later," my team member spoke, and I nodded again.

I had not even registered that he too was holding his bag now. Shlok led me to his car and forced me to sit in it.

"Where do you live?" he demanded as he pulled up the 'Maps' app on his phone. I gave him the address and he started to drive.

"I won't let you step out of the car until you tell me what happened," Shlok hissed as he drove us out of the premises.

"Roshesh is a perverted bastard," I spoke hoarsely.

"That is well known; you are too new to know it though," he shrugged. "I never liked you talking so cozily with him. I never liked him personally."

"Is it why you stopped his promotion?" I spoke.

"Umm, not that I should tell you, but I stopped his promotion because he did not build a strong case. Very rarely does it happen but the entire panel was against his promotion, this year and last!" he informed.

"So what did he do to you? Did he say anything inappropriate?" he asked seriously.

"If only I could tell you," I sighed.

"But I thought you could tell me anything," he insisted. "I thought we…" and he paused.

"We are nothing," I gritted my teeth. "You are just my manager!"

"And as that scene happened on the floor, I, as your manager, demand to know about it," he spoke with a hint of irritation.

"I choose not to tell you," I spoke. I didn't know what this would do to us, or even there was an 'us', but I could not just break his heart by telling what Roshesh wrote in that paper!

"Fine," he snapped, and he accelerated. He did not stop again until we were outside the society I lived in. Without another word, he unlocked the car and waited for me to step out.

"Shlok," I whispered. He did not look at me, so I just placed my hand over his, which was resting on his knee, and squeezed his hand in my own. "Be careful. You are successful, and most people don't get motivated by your growth, they don't see how hard you have worked to be where you are, they see it as a source of jealousy. And believe me, people can do nasty things when they are jealous."

"Don't you think I know it?" he snapped.

"Just be careful, I would hate it if you were to get hurt," I whispered.

"And you? What did he do to you?" he demanded. "He did something to you to hurt me, isn't it?"

"He did not do anything to me," I sighed.

"Don't lie to me," and he hissed so angrily that a shiver ran down my spine.

"He knows that I like you, so he is using it to hurt me, that's what happened, isn't it?" he demanded.

And my jaw dropped.

"Have you been telling people?" I started.

"I am not stupid, Nyra. You have no idea who my father is, my step-father, I mean… why do you think I am unmarried and single until now? You don't know anything about me. And if it got out that I… I…" and he paused to draw huge breath, as he grabbed my hand in turn and intertwined our fingers together.

"You are scaring me," I whispered.

"Don't be scared, Nyra. I won't let anything happen to you. My Nyra," and he spoke the last two words so softly that it just took my breath away.

And while I did not reveal till the end what that bloody Roshesh wrote on that paper, I couldn't help but notice the aura that was radiating from Shlok's every being.

And as I got into bed that night, holding tightly to my children as I felt epically scared of losing them, I realised that maybe, inadvertently, I may have fallen for a man who would be the downfall of my entire being. And as I pressed Shiv and Ojha's sleeping forms to my body, I promised myself; no matter what happens, nothing will ever come in between their happiness and health. I maybe a mere woman without any power, but I am a mother, and there is no bigger protector in this godforsaken planet than a mother.

25 RESOLVE THAT BROKE ME!

The next morning I woke up late, like usual on a Saturday, but today, Dhruv was quite agitated. I was not sure what was wrong with him, so I waited for him to speak up, but Dhruv being Dhruv, did not say anything, but continued to lash out, even if mildly. The problem with people who never get angry is, a slight raised voice hurts like hell. And this mild lashing out had both children quivering beside me.

"Would you tell me what is wrong?" I demanded.

Dhruv looked at me and two possibilities flashed in front of my eyes. First, he knew about what Roshesh did, and thought what was written on that paper as true. Second possibility was that someone had seen Shlok and me sitting in his car out by the society gate and had fed Dhruv some rubbish story. In between the two, I don't know where my chances were better, but what he told me, after almost an hour, was actually worse than both combined situations.

"Kids summer vacations are starting next weekend," Dhruv spoke with a sigh, and I realised what the hell he meant.

"No!" I whispered, "You know I can't!"

"They called last evening," Dhruv rubbed his face and looked at me.

"And?" I asked, trying very hard to reign in my anger.

"Like every year, they want us to visit Lucknow," and he dropped the bomb.

"Like hell we are," I growled. "Have you forgotten the shit fest they pulled this time when they came here?"

"Well, they are old, they are entitled to their opinion, it does not mean we need to sever ties with them," he reasoned.

"Fuck that," I shouted.

"Nyra," he hissed, "language, or have you forgotten you have two children in this house?"

"They are not here, are they?" I retorted. He very well knew I never used any foul words in presence of our children, and at present, both Shiv and Ojha were playing in their own playroom.

"Still," he grimaced.

"Are you fucking kidding me?" and I laughed. After the day I had yesterday, the last thing I had expected was another fucking hailstorm in my own home. Whatever maybe the situation in our home, I at least never felt attacked directly in here, not unless his parents came!

"Every year since Shiv was born, we go to Lucknow for a few weeks. We both take leaves—" he started.

"No," I bellowed. "You DO NOT take leaves, I take leaves, because their precious son can work from home in Lucknow, but the maid daughter-in-law of theirs cannot. She has to be turned into a freaking barbie, covered in powder and donned in makeup and jewellery from head to toe like a show doll, and is to be present to do everyone's bidding, including the neighbours, all day long."

"You are blowing it all out of proportion," he heaved a sigh.

"Oh, shut up, Dhruv," I ranted on, "tell me once you have been forced to do something you did not wish to! Be it my parents' home or your own. You are a prince of your own house, and precious '*kunwar-sa*' in my parents' home," I paused to let him react, but he did not. *Kunwar-sa* was the normal respectful title that was given to the sons-in-law in a typical Rajasthani household. As Dhruv just stared at me like I was being ridiculous, I continued, "But do you even remember what your parents have done to me? Your mother knows I cannot wear bangles for a longer duration, remember when she forced me to wear two dozen metal *chudi* in each hand, and my hands were so swollen that you had to cut those metal *chudi* with a wire cutter? And when you did that, the kind of fit she had thrown?"

He did not reply, of course, how could he. He too knew I was right. But I thought maybe another experience will help him remember, "Or did you forget the time when your mother forced me to wear toe rings? A few weeks after I had returned from the hospital. You yourself put them on me because I could not bend that much back then, remember? How touchy feely she was that I was not wearing them! And when my toes had swollen twice the size, and—" I inhaled heavily as the memory of those emotional tortures brought tears to my eyes, "…and when my toes were brutally cut and blood oozed out of my wounds, she still did not let me get rid of them? Do you remember my crying and begging you to take them off, but you hesitated. I do not forget, Dhruv, you had hesitated. Over her stupid orthodox believes, you had hesitated to acknowledge and support me in my actual pain."

"Fine, they are monsters, so what can I do?" Dhruv snapped. "Should I disown them? Do you want their only child to stay away from them?"

I swallowed angrily. Of course, I did not want that. No matter what, I would not want my kids to make me a pariah, why would I pray such a thing on them. But I, to be honest, would not hurt Shiv's wife so much. I would respect and love her like I would love and respect Ojha.

"I don't want you to disown them or whatever, but with the stunt they pulled last time they were here, I am not going to Lucknow, Dhruv," I whispered as quietly as possible.

"But I will," he insisted. "Nyra, they are my parents, I cannot hurt them so much."

"And what about me?" I demanded. "My feelings don't matter to you, do they? Well, you have shown me as much over and over, but are you going to do this to me?"

"You can go to Jaipur," he suggested.

"Without you and children? Do I need to give my parents heart attack? They are still recovering from Myra Di's divorce. You think that I want them to know that our marriage is over too?" I sighed.

My sister, Myra, had been in an abusive marriage for years on end. And only two years ago she had found the courage to speak up and got free. She was living with her twelve-year-old son now in Delhi, happily. But of course, our parents were not happy. Being old school, they believed that being divorced was the worst fate. Little did they know that being trapped in an unhappy marriage was much, much, so much worse! Well, case in point, me!

"I promised mom we will be there next weekend," Dhruv informed flatly. "You know I cannot back out on my promise."

"And what about promises to me?" I asked, now tears streaming down my cheeks.

"Which promise did I ever break to you? I care for you, I do everything for you. I prioritise your career, I make sure you have everything. What did I not give you?" he asked sourly.

"When you stopped touching your wife, when you stopped having sex with her, when you stopped loving her, seeing her the way you should, you broke every promise you ever made to her!" I whispered. "I have been begging you to take us on a vacation for eight, no hell, nine years, Dhruv, we have not been on a vacation ever since I got pregnant with Shiv. Dhruv, if ignoring your wife, not paying her any attention is the definition of love and promise to you, then I do not want your love and promise."

And the discussion was closed.

But on the following Saturday, I went to the cold empty bed, Dhruv had packed up almost a month's worth of the kids' stuff and left for Lucknow that afternoon. That night, alone in bed, I realised something. I was stuck in this house only because of my children and no one else. After everything we had been through over the course of years, I just could not believe that he left me alone in the house to be with his parents. His parents… who had always neglected and tortured me, have always demeaned me, and have never respected me. And as 'Reached safely' message popped on my phone from Dhruv, another resolve firmed in my heart. And before I could shake that resolve and bring some sense to my mind, I picked up my keys, and walked out of the home.

WHERE I BELONG 26

I drove with tear filled eyes. And no, I did not drive aimlessly, I drove with a destination in my head. And to anyone, who had glimpsed what was really in my mind and heart, it would not be a surprise because, within an hour I was climbing up the elevator to the floor where he lived.

'Maybe it was a mistake,' I thought as I waited at his door for an incredibly long minute. But then I pressed the doorbell and I waited for a few minutes.... The door opened, and holy shit! A girl opened the door, who was wearing a rather short shorts and a tank top!

"Yes," she asked as she looked at me from top to toe.

Fuck! He had another girl over. Fuck! Fuck! Fuck!

"Wrong house, I guess," I muttered as I turned tail and rushed to the elevator to call it. But it was already heading down. Fuck! Now I have to wait. Should I use the stairs. Damn it! I should have used the staircase because his voice came from inside, asking, "Who is it, Sheena?"

I turned around, horrified.

"Some weird girl," Sheena muttered.

But I just dashed to the stairs and started climbing down the stairs. I could go down two floors and then wait for the elevator. Or maybe, I could climb down all seven floors, and hope some of the humiliation and embarrassment would burn from within me.

"Who?" his voice came from a floor above me.

And as I looked up, his face was peering down at me.

"Nyra?" he looked confused.

I just closed my eyes and shook my head.

"Wait, Nyra," he called, but I was already dashing down the stairs.

I practically flew all the way down, and as my car was parked in the basement, I did not stop on the ground floor, where, maybe I hallucinated, he was there. But how could he already be there!

I climbed down more, but very slowly now as I was practically panting. And my legs were shaking so violently that I knew I would have to sit in my car for at least good thirty minutes before I could even drive myself home. But what home was it? Where did I even belong to? I did not have anyone. My husband, my apparently perfect husband, took my children to his parents' place, parents who already had disowned me. My parents, who should always support me, actually love my husband more than they love me, and they would disown me even for thinking about divorce. And Shlok, the man who had called me 'My Nyra' only last week, was warming his bed with another girl named Sheena.

With tears still flooding my eyes, I now walked straight into Shlok's arms.

"What's wrong? What are you doing here?" Shlok demanded.

"I am a fool," I cried, now unable to even stand up straight.

"What?" he asked, confused as he helped me stand straight.

"I am leaving. I did not think twice, I just…" I choked.

But Shlok must have noticed how violently my body was shaking because in one swift motion, he lifted me in his arms—bridal style.

And as my eyes widened in horror, he smiled.

"You look like you would fall any moment," he spoke simply.

"Put me down, please," I spoke, unable to stop the very different kind of shivers that were running up and down my spine. No one, literally, no one had held me in arms ever. Dhruv never even tried to take me in his arms, not even when I was slimmer and weighed much lesser. "You will hurt your back, please put me down!"

"Well, if you would fight or make sudden moves, then maybe I will hurt my back. But you are not that heavy, Nyra," he smiled. "Now, would you call the elevator, let us go up and talk."

"I want to go home," I sniffed.

"I am taking you home, My Nyra." And he spoke with such sincerity that I could not even contradict him. I just pressed the elevator button, and we went upstairs.

And this time, in his home, he did not take me to the second room, but he placed me in his own bed. "Err, Sheena is taking that bed, so, would you mind sharing mine tonight?"

My eyes widened at this. And I was not sure what shocked me more? Was it the prospect of sharing bed with him or that Sheena was not sleeping in his own!

A knock on the bedroom door stopped whatever was brewing in my head.

"Are you the same Nyra about whom my brother has been talking for so damn long?" Sheena asked in a dramatic way.

My eyes flitted to Shlok's face at this. "Brother?" I whispered.

"Yep, did I not tell you that my sister was visiting?" he spoke thoughtfully.

I just shook my head at this.

"Must have forgotten in everything that went on the other day," he shrugged.

"By the way," Sheena continued, "what was in that paper anyway? You did not tell him, mind telling me?" she asked with raised eyebrows.

"Sorry, my sister does not have any manners," Shlok rolled his eyes.

And the way Sheena flicked her finger in his direction, I knew he was right. This girl literally had no manners.

"Well?" Sheena demanded.

And I just shook my head. Shlok gave his sister a 'leave now' kind of look, and Sheena left muttering something to herself.

"Have you eaten something tonight?" he asked in such a loving tone that I melted.

I just shook my head.

"The cook made chicken, but I guess that is out of question for you, isn't it?" he asked thoughtfully. "How about I order you a pizza?" he asked.

I shrugged, and at this, he placed his hands on my legs and felt the tremors. "I know what running down those flights of stairs must have done to you, so rest up. I will be back once pizza is here, alright?"

I nodded.

"Don't be asleep when I am back, alright. I need to be out or Sheena will be in here. And out of both options, I think me out there is a better one," he grinned.

I nodded my head. Because no matter what, I did not know what to make of his sister. She was weird as hell! And why the fuck she had that pompous brat kind of attitude?

At my nod, he got up and started to walk out. But then he came back, bent down, and planted a kiss firmly on my cheek, making my eyes widen with shock.

"Now we are even," and giving me a very cocky grin, he stepped out.

I clasped my cheek and sat there motionless for a long time. His sudden kiss had spread different kind of jitters all over my body. And deep down, I liked them.

As I slipped in his bed, engulfed in his scent and warmth, savouring the feel of his blanket, for the first time in a long time, maybe ever in my life, I felt a combination of relief and guilt. Guilt because I was in another man's bed and I liked it, but relief because if I remove the guilt from the equation, every ounce of my being wanted to be here. As if this was my home after all. As if, this was where I belonged.

27 SOME DANGEROUS BAGGAGE!

I woke with a start. He had told me not to fall asleep, but I did. And as I woke up, the first thing that I realised was my whole body was covered in a blanket, even my face. And the scent that was flooding my senses was not my own. Also, the sound that filled the otherwise eerie quiet was not of snores that often plagued my night's sleep, but it was rather a steady rhythm of deep breathing.

I peeked out of the blanket and found Shlok sleeping beside me. He was wearing a t-shirt and had another blanket covering him up to his waist. The lights were on in the dressing room so that the room was not dark. But the door was closed tonight. Was it because of me, or was it open last time because of me?

I looked around and found my phone on the nightstand. The time was 4AM. And there was a message from Shlok saying pizza was in the fridge if I wanted to eat it. And as if on cue, my stomach grumbled. Why won't it? I had not eaten since breakfast the previous day, because post breakfast Dhruv had told me that he had booked three seats on a train to Lucknow, and he was leaving with children, *my children,* post lunch. Of course, post that declaration I could not swallow another bite. Dhruv had already told the kids that I cannot join them because I had to go to office almost daily for the next two weeks. And it would be best for them to go to Lucknow and be with their grandparents!

Shiv had asked me rather glaringly about my two weeks office thing, and why did I not tell him before? But well, how could I when their father had outright lied, and had not told me about this lie before. But I went along with it. Well, what could I do? But Dhruv promised me that the kids would be back in three weeks' time, and he even showed me return tickets to assure me. But all this did not stop tears to flow. And it did not stop me from breaking down on the floor the moment they had stepped out to take the cab!

I stepped out of Shlok's room slowly and found the house in darkness. Of course, it was dark, it was four in the morning. Flicking on the torch on my phone, I found my way to the kitchen and flicked the lights on. Popping two slices of pizza in the microwave, I waited.

"Are you playing with my brother?" a voice asked from behind me.

I turned around and saw Sheena standing there. She was still in the same clothes, minus the bra as I could see her firmed up tits poking from her tank top.

She raised her eyebrows as she noticed my gaze, and asked, "Are you like one of the insufferable princesses he often dates?"

I was stunned by this. Because insufferable I maybe, sometimes I chose to be that, but princess I had never been. Nor have I been accused of being one as well.

"While I am not a princess, I feel you for sure are a pompous bratty bitch," I rolled my eyes.

She stared at me for a moment, then laughed out loud, so raucously that I practically jumped.

"Well, why do I feel you are not like the other girls my brother has dated," she assessed, "but you seem more trouble than them because he seems to like you, like really like you."

I had no answer to this declaration. I was sure that I was in love with Shlok, well, 95% sure, but did he also feel something similar for me.

"So, again, are you here to play with my brother's feelings or are you serious about him?" she demanded, crossing her arms around her rather prominent chest.

Before I could answer her, she continued, "Because if you are, know this, I have picked up a thing or two from my stepdad, and I won't hesitate to use it against you."

"Who exactly is your stepdad?" I asked in shock. Because only the other day Shlok too had mentioned him; and how he was still single because of his stepdad.

"Only the biggest don of certain states," Sheena shrugged. And the pizza slice in my hand dropped. Her eyebrows arched as she asked, "Did my dear old brother did not tell you about our family history?"

"Err..." I did not know what to say. So, I quietly picked up the pizza slice and reheated it.

"But if he did tell you about us, you won't be here, like the other girls or boys, for that matter," she rolled her eyes, "who do not stay in long term relationships with us."

"What do you mean?" I asked, now panicking. My hunger had vanished now, replacing it was fear, absolute fear.

"I will let my dear old brother tell you about it, but I am going to bed now...." she grinned and walked away.

"Oh, brooo..." and she shrieked at Shlok's bedroom door, "your girl would run away, so better catch her!"

And as I groaned under my breath, I heard hurried shuffling in the room, and I could swear Shlok had literally jumped out of his bed to come out.

"Are you leaving?" he asked suddenly as he stood at the bedroom door.

"I wanted to eat something," I replied with a smile, popping my head out of the kitchen "and I am certainly not going to leave at–" I checked my phone, "around 4:30 in the morning." And I don't know what he was thinking, but the way he was looking at me, in his sleepy state, with such vulnerable look, that I could not help but lift an arm to call him to me. And for a moment he just stared at me, but then, he rushed forward and hugged me with all his might. He hugged me so tightly that I was practically lifted from my feet. It took me a moment to register the warmth that was flooding in my body at his touch, but then, before he could release me, I hugged him back. And the moment my arms wrapped around his body, I felt him relax. He dipped his face in the crook of my neck, and I felt complete.

I don't know for how long we stood there like that, but it seemed like neither of us wanted to let go.

Ahem! Hem! Of course, Sheena had to clear her throat to interrupt. "Umm, you guys know there is a perfect bed for that sort of thing and more in there, right?"

Shlok pulled back and I was amazed to see he had tears in his eyes. I wanted to ask him what was wrong? Was hugging me so awful? My God, was this why Dhruv never hugged me? But before I could ask him anything, Sheena continued, "Umm… senti much," she rolled her eyes, "but if you love birds can move your huggy-buggey somewhere else, I would like to get a bottle of water."

And feeling embarrassed, Shlok led me to his bedroom.

"What's wrong?" I asked the moment he closed the door and locked it for good measure. I felt a bit uncomfortable when he locked it. I mean yes, I came to his house. I let him pick me up in his arms, bridal style, and now I did let him hug me, and well, not to mention, I kissed him before, but, I was not looking for… I mean, how do I tell him.

But before he answered me, he pulled me in his arms again and exhaled in such relief that it felt he was getting his breath back with me in his arms.

"The only thing that was wrong was that you were not in my arms," he whispered in my hair. "And believe me when I say this," he continued, "I do not wish to spend another waking moment without you in them."

"Shlok," I whispered, "I—"

"I am not asking for anything else, not until you are ready, believe me, I won't force you," he stiffened in my arms, "but do tell me this, can I kiss you and hold you, for now?"

"Hold me, yes, kiss me on my cheek, forehead, yes," I whispered. I was not ready for a full-on kiss yet.

He pulled back and placed a deep kiss on my forehead, as he inhaled the scent of my hair deeply.

"By the way did you eat, or my obnoxious little bratty sister did not let you eat at all?" he asked with narrowed eyes.

"She is a brat yes, but I don't think she is obnoxious," I smiled and he laughed.

"You are just perfect," and with a smile, he went out and brought back two slices of pizza that I had left on the kitchen counter. "Eat, then tomorrow morning we can talk about what is wrong at your home," he spoke as he literally pushed a slice of pizza in my mouth.

"What made you say so?" I asked, chewing, and he raised his eyebrows the way I love so much.

"Why on earth were you at my doorstep, unannounced, in tears? I am sure your husband or in-laws, umm, scratch that, actually I am sure both your husband and in-laws did something horrible that made you leave your kids behind," he finished. But I did not reply to this.

And as we went to bed that morning, it was almost 6AM now, I realised that this man, this mysterious, strange man knew more about me than my own bloody husband, to whom I had devoted almost half my life. And while Shlok came with challenges, and as per Sheena he did seem to come with some dangerous baggage, I wanted to spend the rest of life, or as much I would get to spend in his arms, getting to know him.

BITE ME IN THE ASS! 28

I woke up the next morning feeling incredibly relaxed. Recently I had started reading too mushy, too sexy werewolves stories… well, I had gotten a contract with an online platform to write a story there and I needed to know the nuances of that world, and in that made up world, the 'mate bond' was very strong.

The stories showed that the *fated mates* were perfect for each other—like their souls were one—the literal version of Hindi dialogue, '*do jism, ek jaan,*' types you know, and that around them, in their bed, the mate felt the most relaxed. And while some mates had chosen mates, they were nothing in comparison to the fated mates.

And this morning, waking up in Shlok's bed made me feel like he was my fated mate; like in his arms the part of my soul, which I didn't even know I was missing, was snapped back and I was whole again. And somehow Dhruv felt like my chosen mate. Was it possible for mere humans too? I wondered as I got up and walked to the door to see where my dream mate was!

"I think she would leave today," Shlok was saying.

"But why is she here, out of the blue? I did not even know you had a relationship with her. I actually thought you were involved with that Grisha chick from your office," Sheena spoke.

And I felt like a punch in the gut. I knew this Grisha chick. She was the one with whom Shlok always talked so flirtatiously. The same girl I had seen him laughing with before.

"Yeah, Grisha is… well… not important," Shlok spoke abruptly, and Sheena snorted.

"And this girl is?" Sheena demanded.

"She actually is," Shlok sighed.

"So, you are going to make it formal with her? Is she the one?" Sheena's shock was evident even when I was eavesdropping on their conversation.

My heart thudded strongly at the last words.

"She is—" Shlok trailed off. "It is complicated with her, Sheena."

"Duh! If it weren't complicated, she won't be the one. Nothing comes easily with people like us, does it?" Sheena sighed. "And you haven't told her about our dear old dad, isn't it?"

And I could tell it was not a question, but a mere observation.

"You think she would be here if she knew?" Shlok demanded.

"But she deserves to know, if there is a chance of her getting poisoned or worse, she needs to know," Sheena insisted, and my jaw dropped.

What the fuck was this? I wondered. I wanted to barge in there and demand answers but at that moment my phone rang, almost giving me a heart attack. It was a video call from Dhruv.

I quickly fixed my hair, and I walked out to the balcony to take the call.

"Mom," Shiv spoke, and my face split in a wide grin. "Why did you not come with us?" he demanded.

"Hey, darling, how are you?" I asked. "How is *dadi's* home?"

"Fine," he rolled his eyes dramatically.

"Are you having fun?" I asked, tears threatening to pour out.

"Yeah, we are going to the market today," and he said in such an insufferable tone that I almost laughed. "Why are you not here? Why are you in office for two whole weeks?"

"Sorry love, I had work," I sighed.

"Not fair, mom, you chose work over us," he accused.

"Who said it?" I demanded.

"*Dadi* did," he shrugged.

And it infuriated me. Not just Dhruv lied to the kids to bring them to Lucknow, now his parents were poisoning them against me. How dare they!

"Actually, darling," I growled, "I wanted to be with you, but dad knew I had to go to office sometimes… I asked him to stay so that we all can stay home together, with me going to office sometime or other, but well, dad wanted to go home. He was missing his parents, so he took you with him."

Shiv twisted his mouth at this.

"I would never choose work or anything or anyone over you, you know that, right?" I insisted.

And when he did not reply, I asked him, "Who am I to you?"

"Mom," he spoke in a bored voice.

"And for a mom, who is the most, the most important person in the world?" I asked seriously.

"Children," he sighed.

"So, how can I choose work over my children, you tell me?" I asked in a pleading voice.

And he exhaled in relief.

"What should I do?" he asked me now, confused. Oh, my little boy. My beautiful, adorable, little boy.

"Dad was missing his parents, and they are your grandparents, so you all should spend time with them. But know this, your mom loves you the most, okay?" I stressed.

"I love you too, mom," he smiled, finally. And my heart relaxed.

"I miss you," I choked.

"I miss you too," he nodded.

"Where is Ojha?" I asked.

"Dad said she should not talk to you as she would cry. She had been asking for you, a lot… like a lot. She cried too, so dad asked me to take the call separately," Shiv informed, and my eyes welled up. Oh, my poor baby. She was only four years old, soon to be five, but she was little. And she needed her mother, so did Shiv, but Dhruv… Dhurv took them away from me!

"That's okay. I miss you both, so much. You both take care, okay?" I spoke sadly.

"Will you come here if you are free?" Shiv asked.

"I cannot, love. I cannot come to Lucknow, but your dad can bring you both back whenever he wants. I may be here or there, but the moment I would know you are back, I will come right away."

"Where will you be?" Shiv asked.

"Work, where else?" I smiled.

Shiv nodded.

"I love you, mom, talk to you later?" he asked.

"Whenever you want to, just call, alright?" I smiled.

And after a kiss in my direction, he disconnected the call.

I sat by the railing of the balcony for a long moment, staring at my home screen where I had a photo of Dhruv and the kids, laughing. But then, suddenly, Sheena came out of the other balcony, raging in fury, "You have kids? You are married with two children and yet you are here, in my brother's bedroom? Oh, you are such a slut!"

I sat rooted to the ground for a moment. Umm, excuse me! But what was it to her? I never hid anything from Shlok, in fact, I had been telling him that we cannot be together… it was him and his words 'My Nyra' that lured me here. Okay, yes, I came here of my own volition, but hello, trying to stay alive here and not die of depression!

"Sorry," Shlok's haphazard face appeared in the balcony next to his sister, and he dragged her back inside. She was shouting, she was out of her mind, and Shlok closed the door shut.

I decided to let the duo deal with their situation while I dealt with mine.

I called Dhruv as I was already upset with Shiv's words, and now too infuriated by the accusation of being a slut!

Well, hello, I was not a slut! If I were, I would have many, too many sexual partners and I would not be inconsolably and horribly sexually unsatiated all the time!

"How are you doing?" Dhruv asked instantly. "Listen, I am sorry for being an asshole before," he started.

Okay, so he was calling himself an asshole, that was a good start, also it meant that kids or his parents were not around. "Oh, yes, you have been, and you are. Why is my son thinking that I chose my work over him?" I demanded.

Silence!

"You cannot stay fucking silent on call, Mr Manchanda, you need to answer me," I hissed.

"Mom…" he just spoke the word.

"And your fucking dad!"

"Language, Nyra. Whatever maybe the situation, they are still my parents, show some respect," he spoke angrily.

"I will show them respect when they do something, anything, to bloody earn it. I want my kids back," I demanded.

"They are mine too," he snapped.

"I know they are your kids, but to hell with your parents. Be their father when they are with their mom," I yelled. "I want my kids back."

"You know what, Nyra," Dhruv spoke in a soft but threatening tone, "I was feeling bad so I was planning to bring them back day after, but now, I will be back after three weeks, maybe four!"

"Dhruv, don't you dare poison my children against me, don't you dare keep them away from me," I screamed. And I could sense that my voice had carried inside because the screams from inside stopped abruptly.

"No," Dhruv spoke calmly now, "I have already spoken to mom and dad about it. Do you think so little of me that I would feed ill things about you to Shiv and Ojha?"

"Not you, but your parents," I spoke softly too.

"Let me deal with them. And you, deal with your shit, Nyra. You need to get your mental health checked, you sometimes lose it. And no need to get enraged, we both know about it," Dhruv commented.

"I cannot believe you are throwing that in my face again! You know very well that I have a traumatic past and that I have triggers, and in our years together it has been you who has been causing those triggers and driving me to the pit of insanity. You know about those triggers for years, I told you after self-reflection. And yet, you have never cared for those triggers," I almost cried. And it was so true. I remember hitting Dhruv with TV remote when I had one of my rage episodes, and then I had spent the whole night trying to understand what made me so angry. And the next morning I had apologised and had shared those triggers with him. And he had promised not to repeat them. Because even he realised that over the years, only three things did something to me that resulted in my incandescent rage. But like everything else, he never fulfilled his promises. And while my rage episodes were limited now, they still happened!

"I will bring kids back safe and sound," Dhruv spoke after a pause. Of course, he did not acknowledge that he did things that triggered my rage episodes....

"Without brainwashing them," I insisted, no I begged this time.

"I promise that," Dhruv assured. "But I will bring them only later. I think living apart will do us some good, Nyra."

And as I looked up, I saw Shlok standing at a distance in his room, waiting for me to wrap up the call. And I knew that the distance was not going to do my marriage any good now, instead the more he stayed away, the closer I would get to Shlok.

"You betrayed me, Dhruv," I whispered. "When you chose your parents over me, after everything they did to me, you betrayed me. I do not know what good your distance would do to us, but I will try, for our children, to live civilly with you..."

"Nyra," he heaved a sigh. "I am sorry, okay."

"Your sorry is not going to do a damn, Dhruv. You should have thought of it when you took my children away from me. I am their mother, you know I do every fucking thing for them. I live for them and yet you took them from me. I would never ask you to stay away from your parents, but who gave you the right to take my children away from me?" I asked solemnly.

I closed my eyes, and I knew deep down the fight to keep this marriage alive was dead in me. It died when Dhruv decided to leave me in tears and go to his parents who had treated me like a maid, no worse, like a slave for years.

"Take these days to think about everything, Nyra, we can talk when we are back," Dhruv spoke sadly.

"I want to talk to my children each day, without fail. As about you, you can choose to talk to me or not, I won't care," and I disconnected the call.

I turned and looked out at the horizon and felt Shlok's arms around my waist.

"Sorry about everything," Shlok whispered in my ears. I just nodded in acknowledgment. "Hungry?" he asked. And I just shook my head.

"What do you want to do?" he asked, making me turn. So many things were racing in my head, and I was unable to pinpoint on one thing.

"Sleep," I groaned, and he chuckled.

He pressed his lips to my forehead, and led me back to his room, and pushed me in the bed. "Here," and he pressed a glass of milk in my hands, "drink this, and then you can sleep some more. I will try to get rid of Sheena by then too," he grinned.

"Don't, she is your sister," I started but he rolled his eyes.

"She is too much sometimes, anyway, she was to leave by evening, a few hours early won't do any harm," and he pushed the glass closer to my lips.

I drank quickly, finally realising how hungry I really was.

As I put the glass down, he raised his hand and brushed my lips with his thumb slowly and sucked it. There was something so seductive in that gesture that I felt a throb in between my legs, but I squeezed them tight. I think, I seriously think he noticed the movement of my legs, because his eyes darkened a bit, showing he too was feeling the same.

"Sleep, you look like you need it. And–" he started to get up but paused, "did I hear it right? Your husband took your children away."

I nodded sadly.

His expressions turned furious at this but he did not react.

"So, it means you can stay here longer?" he asked seriously.

"If you wish me to," I bit my lip, and at this he pinched my chin and pulled my lower lip from between my teeth with him thumb.

I don't know what he planned to do, but he bent down and kissed my cheek, my jaw, my chin, and my other cheek, and then my forehead. And when he pulled back, I could see desires burning in them, quite similar to what was turning my whole body into a bloody inferno.

"If I get my wish, My Nyra, you will never leave this house, like ever," and he blinked rapidly and that desirous look vanished, replaced by a laughing expression.

"Sleep," he poked my nose and left, closing the door behind him.

And as I went to bed, well, around noon today, I knew one thing for sure… if I also got my wish, I would also never leave this house, like ever. But in my wish, I will also have Shiv and Ojha with me, and we four would be one happy family. But as none of my wishes ever came true, like ever from my childhood, I knew even desiring to stay in the comforts of his bed would bite me in my ass, a lot. However, considering everything I have ever done has bitten me in my ass, I would gladly shove my ass in the face of whoever did the biting, if I get to spend some precious, most memorable, and hopefully pleasurable days in Shlok's arms.

29 OF COURSE, I TRUST YOU, DUH!

When I woke up, I saw a packed bag on the side of the bed.

"Are you going somewhere?" I asked Shlok, who was just sifting through his drawer. "And is Sheena home?"

"Ah, yes, I mean, no, Sheena is not home, she left, rather angrily!" he smiled, but then spoke with a nod, "And yes, I am leaving," and he transferred some more things from his drawer to the side of the bag. "And I need my laptop," he added.

My face fell. Didn't he say that I could stay here like forever, did he mean that I could stay here without him?

"Firstly, I am sorry, but I hijacked your privacy a bit," he apologised.

My hands instinctively went to my chest to cover myself. He noticed that gesture and then narrowed his eyes. "Umm, nothing physical, do you think so low of me?"

"Are you getting the British accent?" I asked, surprised, because he used a proper British tone just now.

He shook his head, and then added, "I would not violate you like that, I hope you know me enough."

"Of course," I nodded. "Sorry… so what did you do?"

"I took your phone and sent your team a message that you are going on an emergency leave for a week, and an email to, well, me, that you need a weeklong break," he informed sheepishly. "Sorry, I know I should not have gone into your phone…"

But I just shook my head, unlocked it, and then threw it in his direction. "I have nothing to hide from you," I smiled. But when he raised his eyebrows and slowly raked my body from top to toe, I added, "… in the phone! However, I do not think physically too I have anything to hide from you. Nothing Grisha or your other girlfriends have not shown you already."

And his face turned red at this.

"Grisha is not my girlfriend…" he spoke simply. "We are… I mean we *were,*" he emphasised on the past tense, "… were friends with benefits, that's all."

"And what are we?" I asked curiously.

"That is for you to decide, I am open to any and all titles and suggestions," he laughed.

This time my face turned red.

I looked around, then spoke, "So, why am I going on a weeklong leave?"

"I thought I would take you on a vacation," he smiled.

And my heart trembled. I love travelling; I have been asking Dhruv to take me to places for years on end, but he… well, he…

"I remember you saying back in Mumbai that you love beaches, and while it is not the ideal time, June and all, but I thought we can go to Goa, what say?" and he spoke with such enthusiasm that my heart literally stopped for a second or so.

"Goa?" I asked, shocked.

"Yes, we can stay in the hotel during the day, then we can go to the beach at night, and I would suggest morning, but I have come to realise that you are not a morning person, are you?" and he grinned. "And I have booked a room in a hotel that has a private beach, so we won't accidentally meet any of the office people who may be on workation in Goa, which actually happens quite a lot now."

I stared at him for a moment, and he asked, "Umm, bad plan?"

But I did not reply to him with as many words, instead, I flung myself in his arms and he laughed as he wrapped his arms around my body and lifted me gently.

"I think I need a shower," I spoke as I wrinkled my nose at my own body odour. Of course, I had not bathed for like more than a day now, in middle of June!

"I don't seem to mind it," he pulled back and grinned.

"But I do," I sighed as I dropped back on the bed.

"But we do have a conundrum, isn't it?" he snickered. "While I don't mind you wearing my clothes, like ever. I personally feel you look sexier in them," he grinned, and I blushed, "I think I cannot allow you to be in public looking like that."

"I will go home," I rolled my eyes.

"I can join you," he spoke as he nodded. "Our flight is at 9PM, we need to be at the airport by sevenish, so, we have around four hours for our lunch and your shower and packing. Should we do the needful at your place then?"

I wondered what I would feel with Shlok in my home. Would I feel guilty?

"What was the conundrum?" I asked simply.

He stared at me then spoke, "I do not wish for you to go back there alone, because you may miss your children and feel all those things that made you run away, but I wonder how you would feel having me in your home in absence of your family. So, conundrum, isn't it?"

"You thought so much?" I asked, wide-eyed. "Dhruv never showed slightest inkling of any consideration, like ever."

"Umm," he spoke after a thought, "actually contradictory to many beliefs, men are capable of consideration and thoughtful actions, it's just that we do it only for women we care about."

"So, my husband never cared for me," I spoke sadly. "The man I devoted almost half my life to, never freaking cared for me, is it?"

"I won't go there, but I would say as much," and he cupped my face in his hands and squeezed it gently to make my lips pucker, "I care for you. And I would always care for you…" and he pecked my lips lovingly and dropped his hands.

"Well, I will fix the conundrum for you," he finished as he picked up his bag and opened the door for me to shuffle out behind him, lips still burning with his soft, unexpected kiss, "how about we go to your apartment, you quickly shower and pack for some basics, no need for many fancy things, just things that make you feel comfortable, and then we head out for lunch, and then to airport."

"For how many days?" I asked as he locked the door of his apartment.

"A week for now, when are your kids coming back," he asked, and I halted. A week in Goa with Shlok!

"When are they back?" he asked again.

"Three weeks minimum," I informed simply. The thought of Goa made me miss them even more. I remember making endless plans with Shiv and Ojha about playing on the beach with them, making sandcastles and what not. But Dhruv never took us there. I could take them by myself, but I was scared to take two little children out in a place like Goa. What if some mishap happened?

"I have not booked a return flight yet, we can decide when we want to come back later, sounds good?" he smiled.

"And I am on leave, but you are working?" I asked with raised eyebrows as he sat beside me in my car and buckled his seat belt.

"If we both would go on leave, people would talk. And after that Roshesh's incidence, you are yet to tell what he did by the way, I think you don't want to draw attention to us," he smiled.

"Oh, never," I shook my head. Last thing I wanted people to know that 'I was doing the boss'– which I was not, by the way… yet!

"And besides everything, I think I can skip a few calls, working inactively for a few days and no one would bat an eye, but if you skipped project calls, why do I have a feeling hell will rain fire?" he laughed.

"I wonder how they would manage in my absence for a week too?" I grunted as I drove.

"I already called Vishal and informed him that you have asked for some personal days, so he will cover for you. You may have to cover for him in future, but I did that barter on your behalf," he just shrugged.

"Oh, you are the best," I grinned.

"I have been told," he laughed.

"Now let's go to Goa. Something tells me, we both need this vacation desperately."

And that night, I didn't go to bed. I packed some of my best dresses for the trip, took a quick shower, and then left with Shlok in a cab. We talked all the way through lunch, while waiting at the airport, on flight and as we landed. It was when we landed in Goa and stepped out of the airport, he asked, "Do you trust me, Nyra?" and to this I only replied, "Though it is a bit late to ask me this," I grinned, "… but despite your sister, the threat of getting poisoned or worse—whatever that maybe—knowing I would be one of your endless girlfriends, and about your 'dear old dad', yes, Shlok, somehow, deep down, I do trust you. More than I have ever trusted any man in my entire life, I trust you enough to come to a different city while being fully aware that no one, literally no one from my family or friends know I am here."

30 COLOUR ME EVERYTHING!

"I really need to improve my sleep schedule," I groaned as I turned and saw Shlok on his laptop, while I was wrapped in a thin blanket.

He jerked his head in surprise; he was so engrossed in his laptop that it seemed he had forgotten I was even there. When he turned and grinned at me while placing a finger on those perfect lips, I noticed he had air pods in his ears, and he was on a call.

He raised his hand and showed me five fingers. I nodded and walked into the bathroom to freshen up.

I was still brushing my teeth when he knocked.

"Good morning, sleepy head," he chuckled from the other side.

Once done, I came out, grumbling. "I really need to fix my sleep schedule," I repeated as I looked at the clock. "I just cannot live like this."

"Umm, you can… you are on a vacation," he smiled. "It is just after 2, I was about to wake you up once I was done with the call. Lunch?" he asked.

I sighed as I walked to my bag to pull out some decent clothes to wear.

"Put this on underneath, we can go swimming in hotel's pool later," he spoke as he threw a lace towards me.

"Err..." I spoke as I raised it to my eye level, utterly horrified. "Where is the rest of it?"

"It is a swimsuit," he informed casually.

"Err... no, this is basically being naked in public with very flowery laces around your essentials," I exclaimed.

He pouted. "What kind of swimsuits do you wear?" he asked, confused. "I realised we did not have swimsuits, so I bought this for you."

"I brought my own swimsuit," and I pulled mine out of my bag. It was a full coverall swimsuit, with leggings and sleeves and all.

"You use that kind of swim wear?" he asked, eying my swimming suit.

"Duh!" I rolled my eyes. "And this..." I threw the bikini laces back to him, "I am never gonna wear it."

"You can wear it, sometime," he shrugged, "maybe in the shower!"

Umm, why would I wear anything in a shower, unless... oh! Unless I was with him in it. And I felt my face turn very hot and red at the realization.

"Let us go and have lunch, then maybe we can go swimming fully clothed," I whispered the last words as I rushed to the bathroom to get changed and to save my face, but I left my swimming suit behind as it was not something I could wear under my clothes.

When I stepped out, he was laughing heartily.

"Hey," I slapped him lightly, feeling embarrassed.

So he just raked his thumb on my cheek and whispered, "I like this colour on you."

My mouth hung open at his words and sudden touch. With a lopsided grin, that somehow enhanced his features even further, he pushed my mouth close with his index finger and led me out for lunch.

We had a nice lunch at a restaurant, on a deck, that was overlooking the beach. And it was just blissful. He then went away to take another call, while I just sat in the shade and stared at the rise and fall of the waves.

I was a peaceful sight, and it made me relax. I called Dhruv and had a long conversation with Shiv. He wanted to video call, but I did not wish to upset him. I had promised my little boy that we would come to Goa together, I could not upset him by showing him the beautiful waves. And just like that, I started missing him, them, so much. Why did Dhruv not love me enough to care for me? I wondered as tears started to pour down my cheeks. But I just wiped them hastily. I was dying to talk to Ojha too, but Shiv said that she was missing me a lot and would cry. And I knew he was a good big brother, and if he said she would cry, she would. And last thing I wanted was to hurt my children in anyway. I could run back to Lucknow and be with them… but that would mean living under the thumb of Dhruv's Hitler parents, and I so not wanted it. I wanted to live my life with my children, whether Dhruv wishes to stay in it or not was his choice now!

I was still sitting there, sulking, when Shlok found me again.

"Missing your family?" he asked as he sat beside me in the sand, under the shade.

"How did you know?" I asked, surprised.

"I have started to recognise your expressions. This one," he pointed at my face, "tells me you are missing your kids."

And it hit me. No one, not even my mother ever saw anything on my face. I still remember when I was molested on the road back when I was in college, I had run back home, teary faced. I had spent hours and hours in my room, crying. My face had swollen and turned red; I noticed it when I had gone to the bathroom to wash off the tears, and then I had gone to dinner with my parents. And none of them, neither my mother nor father, saw anything wrong with me. I was so horribly upset, I had been violated and I was sobbing within, but they had not seen it. And neither has Dhruv ever registered if I had cried before I had come in front of him. But here Shlok was, able to see, just in my sad expressions that I missed my children.

"And now you are thinking how much you are amazed by me, and how much you like me," he smiled so broadly that it took my breath away.

"You are wrong this time," I spoke as I wiped my nose with the back of my hand.

"About you being amazed by me, because I am pretty sure I have seen that look on your face every time I have done anything even remotely nice for you," and he laughed. "You know sometimes I feel no one has ever done anything nice for you!"

"You are right about that," I nodded. "No one has ever done anything that showed remotest care or love for me. Not my parents, not my husband. My children have, and I love them for it."

"Okay," and he looked quite uneasy with these words. "What kind of life have you lived, Nyra."

"A total fucked up one," I smiled ruefully.

And he did not respond to it.

"Tell me something," he sighed, and I asked him to continue. "The other day I heard you say to Dhruv that you have triggers that result in rage episodes, what are your triggers?"

"Why?" I bit my lips. Because talking about my triggers also was like a trigger!

"Because I do not wish to do any of them accidentally, Nyra," he added sincerely. And I considered him for a moment. Of course, I cannot lose it with him, he would run away if he saw that side of me! So I started.

"My first trigger is smell of Pan-Masala…" I informed.

"What?" he was confused.

"Not if someone is passing by but up close," I pointed up to my face.

"Why?" he asked.

"My cousin tried to rape me once and he was chewing it, and all of that trauma comes crawling back if I smell pan-masala up close," I whispered, and he stiffened. He grabbed my hand and squeezed it gently to show he understood.

"Tried to? Right?" he asked very seriously.

And I nodded. "I ran away before he could…."

He stayed quiet for a long moment, then asked solemnly, "Okay! Next?"

I swallowed as my breathing changed slightly, "Someone talking while having a wad of something stuck in between their teeth!"

"Also because of your cousin?" he asked.

And I shook my head, "A man molested me in train and he had a wad throughout the journey as he stalked me and then did it! He too was having pan-masala in between his teeth."

His grip on my hand tightened.

"Third?" he asked seriously.

"Mom…" I whispered.

"Meaning?" he was genuinely confused.

"Talking to my mom on any negative thing triggers it," I sighed.

"What do you mean?" he did not understand. No one could unless they knew my history.

"My mom… though I love her a lot, was not a good mother, Shlok!" I whispered. "I have—" and a tear escaped my eyes. "Anyway, that's why I try to be a good mother. I cannot do to my children what was done to me. A mother's actions alter the course of child's future. And whatever my children may do with their lives, I do not want to be the cause of their troubles. From me, they should get a good future."

"You are a wonderful mother, Nyra," Shlok insisted. "I don't think your kids or any kid in the world could ask for a better and loving mother than you. From what I just heard, from what I know, you have been broken so many times. And yet, you have picked yourself up and have mended yourself to be good to your children. Believe me, they would appreciate you in future," he smiled.

And I stared at him with so much awe that I felt my heart constrict.

"That's the look again…" he grinned. "Amazed, huh!"

"Way too amazed, yes," I tried to smile, "but you were wrong before," I sniffled. He arched his one eyebrow questioningly, so I added, "Mr Shlok Rajput, I was not thinking how much I like you, because I do not like you."

And his stunned expressions said it all, so I raised my index finger to stop his reaction, and I added, "I don't just like you, Shlok. I am dead sure that I love you."

No reaction! None whatsoever! He just kept on staring at me, but he did not reply. He did not even blink, he just stared at me.

Well, I was used to this kind of treatment. In the early days of our marriage, I had said 'I love you' to Dhruv quite a few times, but he never responded to it. He just said 'You too' sometimes and I could tell it was out of obligation. And back then I thought he was not the expressive kind because he took so good care of me, but now… after so many years, and with the recent happenings, now I was quite sure that Dhruv just did not love me. Why the fuck did he marry me then? Well, that was a sob story for another day. Coming back to Shlok, he did not say it back, hell he did not even react to it.

That means, he is not in love with me. No big surprises, for all intents and purposes he may have started noticing me only a few days ago! But I have been in love with him for a very long time. Especially considering he had been starring in my dreams for months….

"I think I am gonna take you up on that swimming offer now," I smiled as I stood up.

He just nodded and followed me.

"So, you have any more calls today or are you free now?" I asked him, trying to ease the tension.

"I have a few more calls but we can go for a swim," he shrugged.

"Or, I could stay in the room or go out, whatever makes you comfortable," I stressed. I really did not wish to be a burden on him, which by every step we took, it seemed like it.

"Sure, whatever makes you happy," he replied as we reached the room, and I rushed to the solace of the bathroom. Holy shit! What did I do? I broke Shlok….

Okay, so my parents did not love me, I thought it was not my fault, considering I was the kid there. My siblings hate me, like literally, I know it is not my fault there either. I have always done everything my parents had asked of me, well, who can blame me, I always craved their love. And while I never snitched on my sister and brother, they always thought I did. The relationship with my siblings was kind of on mend now but it's still a long way to go, I think. My in-laws loathe me, well, for obvious reasons. My husband does not love me, like I want him to, at least. And now I have Shlok. He, at least, liked me before, enough to bring me here to spend time with me, but now, he also….

Tears welled up in my eyes, but I quickly washed my face. Well, I am at least loved unconditionally by my children, and I am going to do whatever it takes to keep them happy and with me. And to that avail, if I have to swallow my pride and ego and go to Lucknow, then so be it. The thought in itself brought a fresh bout of tears in my eyes, but I washed them too. I would use this time in Goa to decide what I want to do, and then, I would go back. And once in Delhi, I will decide where to go from there!

After inhaling and exhaling deeply at least ten times, to ensure I would not cry again until I was out of the room, I stepped out.

Shlok was typing at his laptop. The moment I stepped out of the bathroom, he looked at my face. But I turned. And keeping my back firmly to him, I picked up my purse and made to head out.

"Hey," he called out. "Where are you going?"

"Just out," I shrugged by the door.

"Okay, don't forget your phone though," he commented.

Damn it! I forgot my phone. How could I forget my phone? I exhaled from my mouth, plastered my highly practiced smile and turned to face him. He was holding my phone in his extended hand to give it to me, but it dropped the moment his eyes fell on my face.

"Come here," he spoke seriously.

I walked up to him and took my phone. But instead, he grabbed my hand and pulled me beside him.

"I am sorry," he whispered as he placed his chin on my shoulder.

"For what?" I asked simply. Trying really, really hard to not start crying again.

"You know what," he sighed as he wrapped his hands around my waist.

"I want to go around the market. I saw one just across the road from the hotel when we arrived last night," I informed, swallowing a very, incredibly large lump in my throat.

"But I thought we were going for a swim," he sighed again. And his breath brushed on my neck this time, raising goosebumps all over me.

"I suggested I go out; you said I can do whatever makes me happy. I think shopping would make me very happy at this moment," I replied as I wrapped my fingers around his arm and pulled it away. But he did not budge.

"Nyra, you must be used to being alone after crying, but you are not going to be alone now, not at least when you are with me," he spoke sternly.

"I am not crying," I replied as I faced him.

He raised his hand and brushed his thumb on my left eye. And as if on cue, a tear trickled down that eye.

"I know your face, Nyra, My Nyra, and I can tell that you cried," he spoke as he brushed the tear away.

"How?" I choked.

"What how? It is written all over your face, all it needs is someone to notice. You have the worst poker face," he laughed.

At this, more tears leaked my eyes and before I knew it, I was sobbing in his arms, in his chest. He let me cry for a while. He just sat there, keeping me wrapped in his arms, brushing my hair with his hands, caressing my back softly, and at times, brushing my cheeks too. I have never felt this loved before, like I belonged somewhere.

Tina, my therapist from before, suggested a book for me to read that might help with dealing with my past. It was 'How to Do the Work' by Nicole LePera. Although I never finished the book, I followed the author on Instagram. In one of her posts, she mentioned that when someone cries, they should be given space, time, and emotional acceptance rather than emotional monitoring. This acceptance forms the foundation of healthy relationships.

Ironically, I never had this acceptance from my family, but Shlok gave me that. And while I cannot have a desired relationship with him, I knew whatever or however we will end up, it would be healthier than any of my other societal relationships.

"Sorry for making you cry again," he spoke as he rocked me in his arms. "I know why you cried the first time, but for right now, I really don't know what triggered your tears."

I sniffled as I looked at him. He heaved a sigh and pulled out a handkerchief from his pocket and wiped my face.

"No one ever cared to notice," I spoke as my eyes welled up again. He narrowed his eyes at this.

"No one, literally no one has ever noticed when I have cried before," I choked at the words.

"And why does it tell me you have cried a lot," he asked stiffly.

"You have no idea, but what could I do if not cry?" I spoke as I swallowed another big lump in my throat.

"You can leave it to me to make you stop crying," he smiled as he wiped my face yet again.

"Come, let's go for the swim… we can talk then," he started to make me get up, but his laptop started chiming.

"Damn it," he cursed as he turned and looked at the caller. His expressions fell as he saw his screen. I also peered, it was Mihira, our CMO.

"Take the call," I spoke with a smile. "I will go out."

But he just shook his head and pulled me in his arms as he took the call.

"Hey Mihira," Shlok spoke on the call as Mihira's face came on the screen. "Sorry very bad network, cannot turn on the camera."

Mihira's camera went dark too as she said, "No problem, Shlok. How are you doing?"

And they started to talk. I sat beside him and closed my eyes. After a while, he had to let go of my waist to free his hands to work on laptop during the call, but I just shifted and placed my head on his shoulder. He planted a kiss on my forehead as he continued to talk. And his call went on for more than an hour.

And while it was not the usual going to bed, I did doze off because they were talking about things that did not concern me at all. And as I spent minutes suspended in between consciousness and semi consciousness, I realised quite a few things and various shades of colours etched my mind at various realisations. To start with, sadness, I realised that whatever heaven I was living in the moment, it was short lived. Because the man who actually took notice of what I felt and wanted was not mine to keep. And while many other colours like shock, surprise, grief, embarrassment painted my thoughts, the last one was guilt. I felt immensely guilty as a big realisation hit me. A realisation that deep down I was expecting Shlok to say he loved me too, but was it not selfish of me to ask him to love me when I can never truly be his? When in the end, I would leave him for another man. That I would leave Shlok stranded? And it was this colour—the colour of guilt—that made me resolve that during days we would stay here, I would keep my distance from him and would not do anything to make him feel for me. And as much as my heart pained at this, it was actually good that he did not love me. Because our kind of love only ends in pain and loneliness.

31 SLIPPED ME A WHAT?

We had dinner together. It was nice, with just us and few other couples, and live music playing serenely.

"Oh, that is our song," I smiled as the singer started singing …*Ae dil hai mushkil!*

"We have a song?" he laughed with a twinkle in his eyes.

"Oh, in my head we have many songs, different songs represent different things that happened with us, and those songs always remind of those encounters," I smiled sheepishly.

"Oh, really, and what are they?" he asked as he placed his face on his hands and stared at me with amusement in his eyes.

"So, this one, *Ae dil hai mushkil* was playing when we went to your home for that poker night," I smiled. "*Dil ibadat* was playing when we went to your home on that rainy night."

"Okay," his smile getting broader now.

"I was listening to *Teri deewani* and writing when you came running to catch your flight from Bangalore to Delhi…" I smiled sheepishly again. "So that song kind of reminds me when we first met face to face."

His eyebrows rose at this.

"Luca by Suzanne Vega for Mumbai trip," I continued.

"Ahaan," he nodded.

"And *Besharam rang* when you drove me home the other day from office," I laughed. "Stop looking at me like I am a crazy person," I chided.

"I am not looking at you like you are a crazy person, I am looking at you like you are a person who will drive me crazy like hell," he laughed and my breath caught.

But before I could react, he got up and whispered, "Let us make another of your song memories, shall we?" And I was epically shocked. The musician was playing a very soft, slow tune and I did not even recognize it.

"On this music?" I asked as I stared at the musician, who was playing a rather slow, romantic tune.

"Why? Haven't you ever done a slow Waltz or Tango before?" he asked with a grin.

"Duh! All I have ever done is free style and borderline *bhangra,"* and I moved my hands in signature *bhangra* moves.

He laughed but grabbed my hand and led me to a side. "Just follow me," he smiled as he wrapped his arm around my waist and grabbed my hand in his other one and pulled me close to his body. He felt so good against my body that all I wanted to do was lean in and kiss him. But I resisted.

"You took me by surprise this afternoon," he whispered as his gaze bore into mine. I could tell he was feeling vulnerable because the way the gold flecks of his eyes were reflecting in the dim lights, I knew he was feeling too many emotions in one go.

"I am sorry," I whispered. "I spoke too much."

"Hush!" he shushed me. "I thought you said it because you don't truly love me, but because you are misguided. That you are confusing these new budding feelings with love. But, Nyra, I have liked you for months, ever since I first interviewed you, I have liked you. The way you laughed, the way you narrowed your eyes. The way you challenge me, no one does. You are different, and I have liked you since the beginning. But I never could say a thing because you are—" and he paused.

"Married?" I swallowed. And he nodded.

"Would you leave him for me?" he asked, and I stopped moving with him.

"Sorry," he added as he pressed his forehead against mine. "But I want to be with you, always. I want to smile with you, laugh with you. You laugh so easily with me, and you make me smile so often that I cannot express. And I want to take the sorrows away from you…"

"I—" I did not know what to say. "My children?"

"They can live with us," he spoke. "But…" then he paused. "Maybe it would better if they stayed with Dhruv though."

And my face hardened. Why does everyone want to rip my children away from me? The only source of happiness in my life. I am their mother; why is the world so hell bent on my children to grow up without their mother.

"So, you want me, but not my kids?" I asked in a rather accusatory tone.

"I would love to be a father to them," he sighed, "but you don't know the truth about my life. They would be better off with Dhruv or in a boarding school."

My hands dropped from around his body at the last two words.

"Why? Boarding schools are good. Sheena and I were shipped off to one when mom remarried, and we turned out fine," he insisted.

But I could not believe it. If his mother prioritised another man over her children then it was her problem. I would never, never ever prioritise him over my own kids! I would rather die alone than ship my beautiful babies off to some boarding school.

"So, we are at an impasse then," he sighed.

I wanted to know the so-called truth of his life, but hadn't I promised myself that I would not lure him? Make him fall in love with me? So, with a heavy heart I spoke, "But I never said I would leave Dhruv, Shlok. I am sorry if I led you on, but despite whatever happens, Dhruv is the best father in this world. No one can love my children more than him, and—"

"That is what I am saying," he laughed painfully, "be with me, let your kids be with their father."

"A child needs both his/her parents, Shlok," I spoke sadly, "it is killing me that my babies are away from me for three whole weeks, how can you ask me to be away from them forever?"

"We can share custody then, have them once or twice a week, this arrangement should keep them safe," he spoke as he grabbed my face and spoke with such sincerity that it broke my heart. But as words registered with me, sadness was replaced by horror.

"What do you mean by 'this arrangement should keep them safe?'" I demanded, now stepping back from him. Because no matter how madly I was in love with him, I would never put my kids in harm's way.

"Will you ever consider leaving Dhruv?" he asked seriously this time. I looked around and several couples were staring at us. We were now just standing at a side, talking gravely, while the slow romantic music filled the air around us.

"No," I spoke simply. "I am sorry, no matter what happens, I won't take away either of the parent from my children's life."

"Then how does anything else matter, huh!" he demanded, and for the first time, I saw him angry. But I wondered why was he angry? I have not promised him anything. I have never told him that I wished to leave Dhruv. Hell, I have never ever even kissed him properly. Yes, I told him that I loved him but that does not constitute to me saying I would leave the father of my children! Hello!

"What are we, Shlok?" I asked finally.

"I am yet to understand that myself," he huffed as he led us back to our room.

"What are we doing here?" I asked again.

"Trying to figure out what the hell we are to each other," he replied in the same huffy tone.

"I was planning to take you to Goa Fort tomorrow, to break your sleep schedule, but now…" he trailed off.

"I never said that I would leave Dhruv, for me my children have always been first priority," I started again as we reached our room.

"I am willing to be a father to them," he sighed, "but they won't be safe."

"Shlok," I groaned, "with them being my first priority means their safety, their health, their happiness. Their safety is of prime importance to me. I don't know what the problem is with you, but you again and again saying they won't be safe does not really instil any confidence in me, you know!"

"Would you tell me what Roshesh said to you?" he asked suddenly.

"You are comparing my children's security with what that asshole said to me?" I practically shrieked now.

"Actually yes, it is a trade-off between one asshole and another really," he shrugged.

"I do not understand what you mean," I asked sceptically, then suddenly remembering what Sheena had said the other day. "Tell me, Shlok," I asked seriously, "why did Sheena say to you the other day that I should know about your dear old dad, especially considering my chances of getting poisoned or worse? And what is worse than getting poisoned?"

"Trade-off my love, simple trade-off. And don't worry about getting poisoned, I slipped you an antidote yesterday, so even if dear old dad manages to poison you, you would only bleed a bit, you won't die," and with a shrug, he went to the bathroom to change.

And as we went to bed that night, with his hands wrapped around me, his warm breath fanning over me, horror gripped me. What the fuck did I land myself into? If he had to slip me an antidote in anticipation of getting poisoned, what the fuck was his father planning on doing? And why? Oh god, why did I have to land in such a shitty situation? Was my life not miserable enough, you had to add helpings of poison, literal poison to it?

32 WORSE THAN THE 'SOPHIE'S CHOICE'

We did not talk about our relationship again. We woke up, had our breakfast, and while I roamed around, Shlok took a few calls. And before I could get too sleepy, I literally could not sleep last night after he had broken that forsaken news to me, he dragged me to the Goa Fort. We spent the entire day in the fort, which was super fun, if I remove the ever-looming threat over our head. He assured me again and again that his father was not even aware that we were in Goa. For all his father knew, Shlok was in Delhi, but I could not help but keep looking over my shoulder.

But nevertheless, I had great fun. As usual Shlok's company was the best and no matter what our family situation was, in our little bubble, I was incredibly in love with him, and I could not help but cherish every moment I spent with him.

He took just too many photos of us. And while he offered to send them to me, I refused. I had no heart to delete them when I would go back to my unloved life. But I did ask him to mail them to me. Dhruv never checked my emails, well, he never checked my WhatsApp account too, but you never know!

By the time we were back to our room, I was exhausted. We had dinner around 8PM and I was asleep the moment my head hit the pillow.

The next day we went on a boat cruise around a few islands where we swam in the smack middle of the ocean. It was such fun. I could not believe how blue the water was. We came back early from that trip because we were soaking wet, but I did not mind that. We spent the rest of the day in the bed, covered in blankets, talking and eating all sorts of things that room service offered.

The next day we went for a vineyard tour in Goa. Oops, I got drunk with all the wine tasting and he literally had to hold me straight on our way back to the room.

It was our fifth day in Goa and we had spent the entire day in the room. He had back-to-back calls, and while he apologised profusely, I did not mind. I was tired. He did not know it but my legs and my body needed desperate rest after three back-to-back adventurous days. So, I was more than happy to watch Netflix on my laptop while he took calls after calls.

We were sitting in a rather nice restaurant in South Goa for dinner when Mihira called him again.

"Take it," I spoke as his face fell.

"Are you sure? It can be long," he grimaced.

"I am not going anywhere," I smiled at him as I pulled out my ear plugs and showed him Netflix app opening on my phone. "I will watch the next episode while you call, okay?"

Pecking at my cheek lightly, he muttered a quick thanks and sorry, and left.

I was around 10 minutes into the episode when I saw fingers tapping the table next to my phone. Shocked, I looked up, and I recognised the man. I had googled him after Sheena had muttered the words 'only the biggest don of multiple states.'

Dhirendra Singh Rana, man who had married Shlok's mother, aka dear old dad!

I pulled out my ear plugs and gawked at him.

"I see you have recognised me, so should I believe that for once my son actually told a girl who I truly am, or did you just guess?" he asked with such sly grin that all the hair on my body stood on their ends in fear. "Because if it is the first case, then maybe he has finally found the love of whatever little miserable life he has left."

And I just stared at the man. He had dark complexion, round face, bulgy cheeks, huge moustache and a bald patch.

"So, which one is it?" he demanded, now getting impatient.

"He did not tell me about you, I just guessed who you are, found an article about his mother marrying you from an old news site and googled you."

"You are a smart one," and he laughed.

"Am I now?" I asked with a challenging look.

"Listen girl," he pointed a threatening finger towards me, "I eat girls like you raw in breakfast, don't show too much smartness, alright?"

"What do you want from me?" I demanded simply. "Uncle." I added with a bow.

His eyebrows arched up at this.

"You are a feisty one too, I would love to eat you whole," he laughed, "I will make sure to suck at every inch of your body before I take you completely, if you know what I mean!"

I shivered at the thought. Even him mentioning it made me gag and feel violated, but I did not show it. What the fuck was going on?

"I can promise you a better fuck than my son," he shrugged. "Well, at least that's what all his past girlfriends have said to me."

"What?" and despite myself, my anger, my frustration, my disgust showed on my face.

"See girl, you have two choices if you want to be, well, depends on what you choose," his demeanour was so casual that it seemed he was asking about dinner options. He waited for me to ask more, but when I did not, he continued, "You can either sleep with me!" he started, and I fisted my fingers to stop myself from punching him squarely in the face. "Or you could kill Shlok for me."

"What?" I asked, alarmed.

"The choice is simple. If you sleep with me, you will get hefty compensation for each night, and once you have been with me, you won't go back to my loser son, I am sure," he shrugged. My jaw dropped at these words. "Or you can kill Shlok for me. I have been trying to kill him for years, but the promise to his mother always stops me from ordering a direct hit on him or that bloody sister of his. Because whatever maybe the case, I do love their mother, and my word is my bond. And first promise she ever took from me was that I would always protect her children!"

"And sleeping with his girlfriends is protecting them?" I asked, unable to believe it.

"Well, not ordering a hit on them, and keeping them alive for so many years is a form of protection, don't you think?" he asked so innocently that I could not make out what kind of sociopath was he?

"So, what do you choose?" he asked casually again.

"I choose neither," I growled.

"Ah, yes. All girls say this, but then, well," and he put up a thick wad of towel on the table. "Touch it," he ordered.

I did not move.

"Oh, come on girl, it is not a penis! Not yet at least," and he grinned slyly, "just touch it," he stressed.

And despite myself, feeling epically shitty and gross, I touched it. It was a gun, I could tell it, it was a gun.

"I can use this gun on you…" he spoke with a pout. "Or whichever family member you love the most."

And the faces of my innocent children flashed in front of my eyes.

"Those," and he pointed at my face, "whoever you just thought about, those would be gone first. So, who did you think about? Mother? Father? Sister? Brother?" he asked. And it was clear he knew nothing about me. He was just guessing.

"Fine, don't tell me, but do you think I cannot find out within minutes? And if I cannot find who is your dearest, I can kill them all, and be done with it in one go…."

I did not know what I was feeling because I had never felt such dread before. What the fuck was happening here? And why?

"So your choice is clear, sleep with me or kill my son, or I kill everyone you love," and he placed a very small vial on the table which held clear liquid.

"What is this?" I asked in shaking voice.

"Poison, just give it to my son, he would be dead in minutes, easy-peasy," he smiled.

Tears filled my eyes as I stared at the vial. And it seemed I could not breathe at all. He sighed and started to take back the vial, but I grabbed it. He raised his eyebrows as he laughed at my action.

"If you have the guts, then I will find out soon enough that he is dead, won't I?" he smirked haughtily. "But if you don't have the guts, I would be at this beach tomorrow night, alone, waiting for you in a private tent. Leave your phone behind, last thing I want is you recording it to blackmail me. And shave yourself completely before you come, and do not wear any undergarments, I like to get a clear view of what I am fucking," and pushing a note in my direction, he left.

I did not wait for Shlok to come back. Instead, I hailed a cab and went back to the hotel room. After all, who would have the strength to stay in that elegant restaurant after that encounter.

And as I went to bed, I quickly texted Shlok that we needed to talk and I was back in the hotel room. But of course sleep was not to come that night, or for any foreseeable nights for that matter. How could I sleep when I was given choices worse than the Sophie's choice, the ones that were worthy of doom? And while I tried to sleep, hoping it would be a bad dream, but it did not happen. And no matter how much I screamed, cried or hit myself violently, the nightmare did not end. It just kept on going, and going, and going.

33 JUST HIM AND HIS LOVE

Shlok came rushing back to the room, worried as fuck. As his eyes fell on me, he knew something was terribly wrong.

"What happened?" he asked as he grabbed me in his arms and caressed me.

But I pushed him away. Instead, I pulled out the vial of poison from my pocket and put it on the table.

"No," he gasped.

"Yes," I screeched.

"He did not!" he pulled his hair, "Do you know, he is the owner of the biggest chemical factories in North? And that poison is untraceable, and custom-made for me, and so deadly that one swig would be the end," he cautioned.

"No kidding," I growled.

"Did he ask you to kill me with it or else…?"

And this was too much for me. I stood up to my full height and swung my hand so fiercely that the slap that sounded in the room echoed infinitely. Shlok was stunned.

"You knew," I raged, "you fucking asshole, you knew your father would ask me either to kill you or fuck him, and if I did not comply, he would kill my family?" I demanded.

"Yes, that's what he does with all my girlfriends, that's why I only have casual relationships," he almost sobbed.

I grabbed his collar and shook him harshly.

"You knew you were risking my life, my family, my children, and yet you… you are risking my children, Shlok! Why didn't you just whore me out to your father, after all, that is what is your intention, isn't it?"

He grabbed my shoulders and swung me so hard that my back hit the wall, "How dare you?"

"No, how dare you?" I shouted. "You know I won't kill you, I cannot kill you. I love you, you asshole. How can I kill you? Of course, I would not let him hurt my kids, then what is the option for me?"

His eyes softened at this.

"Tell me the truth before I really poison you, what is the deal with your pervert dad," I demanded.

"You can poison me or yourself, it won't matter. Sheena and I take antidotes weekly. And keep them on us always for instant consumption," he laughed.

"What is going on?" I asked through gritted teeth.

He heaved a sigh and then started, "My, well, that pervert bastard is my mother's husband. He loves her, that's true, but he just loves two people; my mother and his son, Dinesh. I told you we were carted off to boarding school a month after their marriage, but his son stayed with them always."

"Son?" I asked, confused.

"Did I not tell you my younger brother lives with my parents?" he spoke, and I nodded. "Well, he is actually my stepbrother. He is Dhirendra Singh Rana's biological son, but he too is a bastard, I mean a literal bastard," Shlok snorted. "Rana never married Dinesh's mother. Dinesh's mother was married to someone else, but had a son with Rana…. Rana is known for his affairs with women, especially the ones he has no right to—those engaged or married to others."

"Okay!"

"Well, Dinesh, my stepbrother, is my stepdad's blood, and in the eyes of Dhirendra Singh Rana, blood matters above all.

Do you know Rana is so powerful that the road on which our house is built is called Rana Road?"

I just blinked in shock.

"Yeah," Shlok snorted. "And as per Rana's will, half of everything goes to Dinesh, and other half goes to his wife, meaning my mother."

I did not react, I just stared. I wanted him to continue speaking and his pauses for my reactions were irritating me.

"My mother's will says everything she owns will be divided amongst all three children, she does not distinguish between the three of us," he snorted again.

"Okay?" I asked impatiently.

"Once wills were made, Rana approached me and Sheena and told us quite clearly that under no circumstances we were to get married and have any child. Because while he cannot kill us, owing to his promise to our mother, he would kill our partners and future kids, if any came into existence."

"And you mom is okay with it?" I asked, aghast.

"Mom doesn't know. He told us making sure she never found out. Even Dinesh does not know… Dinesh is not that bad, he is a decent enough guy, who does not know what his father's ulterior motives are."

"But why?" I asked.

"Because if we died single, there would be no one to inherit our share of his property. We lived hand-to-mouth before mom married him. We were in a very bad shape. And all the money we got was from him. Blood money, yes, but money, nonetheless. And he wants that money to stay in his bloodline."

"But you don't want that money, I am sure you earn a lot," I exclaimed.

"As if I have not told him that. I am rich enough to buy half of yesterday's island, but he does not believe me. Because while I am a multi-millionaire, of my own accord, I am billionaire with what I inherit from him," he sighed.

My jaw dropped at both references. He was a billionaire, and here I was, not even a multi-thousandanaire, if that was even something!

"Can't you tell your mother to write you both off from her will?" I pleaded.

And he laughed. He actually laughed.

"Do you think we have not tried that? He slept with my last three girlfriends, Nyra, he slept with them. They were never the same! He killed two of Sheena's boyfriends. She kept her second boyfriend a secret, hell, I kept you a secret, and yet the bastard found you."

"And yet you brought me here?" my eyes teared up again.

"You were a forbidden fruit, Nyra. I thought he would find out about you and know I would never be serious with you. So, there was no threat to you," he spoke with folded hands. "Believe me I would never do anything to hurt you."

"But he did not dig into my life, thank God or he would have threatened my children," I shouted. "He threatened me. He either wants me to kill you or serve myself to him on a platter, oh, and he wants me to shave myself completely and not be wearing any undergarments when I go to him."

"You will kill me, but you won't go to him, Nyra," Shlok hissed. "I would rather die than see you in the hands of that monster."

And when I snorted, he said, "You would go to him instead?"

"Do you even know how much I love you," I shouted.

He blinked, so I added, "I love you so much that you have been starring in my dreams for almost a year. For a year, a bloody fucking long year, I have been waking up to the sound of your laughter. I love you so damn much that every time I even blink, I see your face. Your touch puts me in a hormonal overdrive, the one I never even knew was present in me...."

He did not respond to this. It was as if he was just registering my words.

"I cannot kill the man I have been in love with for months on end. So…" and as I trailed away, his expressions turned horrifyingly furious.

"And what about me? What about my love?" he yelled.

"What?" I asked, now more shocked than before.

"I love you, Nyra, more than you can imagine. Why do you think I—why do you think I brought you here? I have been in love with you for a long time… you have no idea what staying away from you has done to me. You have no idea what I have done to get over you. And if you were not married, I would have run away with you. I would do anything for you, and if dying is what I need to do to keep you safe, then I would die for you."

And this was too much for me. I rushed forward and kissed him furiously. As my lips met his, I felt I was home.

And as we went to bed that night, kissing hungrily, moaning passionately, with his hands all over me, with him on top of me, around me, beside me, inside me, I knew if this was the last night I had of peace and sanity, then I would spend it making love to him over and over again. Because even though life was throwing me one curveball after another, he was the only straight thing that made sense to me. Just him and his love.

34 A MOTHER, A LOVER, AND SOMETHING ELSE

One week later!

Dhruv called that he was coming home that day. But I was already home, sulking about what I had to do, and dreading the repercussions of the same.

"Mommy," Shiv and Ojha rushed in my arms as I waited for them downstairs outside our building. Both of them started crying in my arms. I tried to pick them both up but couldn't. Not because I did not have the strength, but because of how filthy I felt within.

"Oh my God! You both have grown up so much, I cannot even lift you," I faked a laugh. And they both started ranting about how tall and heavy they have gotten.

"I am sorry," Dhruv huffed as he stared at me.

I nodded in his direction. How could I blame him for what he did because it was nothing in comparison to what I had to do! I could not even look in the eyes of my children, my husband, because the deeds I had done were just beyond comprehension.

And yet, we grabbed their luggage, which was twice as much they had taken, and went upstairs.

"It seems you have done a lot of shopping," I chided my kids.

"Oh, we bought whole shops," Shiv laughed.

"That is good, I cannot wait to see what you guys bought. Hope you bought somethings for me too," I grinned.

"We bought so many things for you," he laughed again.

We started opening things they had purchased, and we laughed and talked and had a lot of fun. We stayed awake till late, but when the kids were finally asleep, Dhruv started.

"I am sorry, I should not have done that," he spoke softly. "I promise to be a better husband from now on."

And as he tried to grab my hand, I walked out of the room where kids were sleeping and went to the other room. He followed me quietly.

"I am sorry too," I whispered.

"You don't have to be sorry," he smiled. "My parents…"

"I love you, Dhruv, always have, but I think our love is platonic. We are best friends," I sighed.

"Are you asking for a divorce?" he asked directly. "Because if you are, think about our children!"

"I am not asking for a divorce, but if you knew what I did in the past two weeks, you would ask for one, I am sure," I sighed.

"No matter what you did, I would never ask for a divorce," he promised. "You are right, we are not sexually compatible, but we are perfectly compatible parents of two wonderful children. And no matter what happens, I swear, I would stay by your side."

"Hold your promises until you have heard what I did," I inhaled heavily, as I continued, "I went to Goa!"

"Explains the tan," he shrugged as he pointed at my face.

"And I kissed someone," I added, carefully reading his expressions.

"Kissed?" he asked with narrowed eyes.

"Yes, and slept, once, I mean for a night," I added. Calling what I did with Shlok that night could never be counted as once!

His lips were pressed in a fine line, as he sat back straight, his shoulders rigid. But then his shoulders slumped as he spoke with his head in his hands.

"I forgive you," he whispered.

I was shocked. I mean I knew my husband was a godsend, but was he really that good and naïve and gullible? Yes, I choose to use those words because this response was proving just one thing, that he really did not love me at all. He did not care if another man ever touched me or kissed me or... but before I could argue, he added, "In the interest of coming clean. Remember, last year when my company took us to a summer retreat in Vietnam?"

And it hit me.

"You slept with someone there?" I asked, trying very hard to control my emotions.

"Yes, Sadhika," he nodded. "We were having a fling, you see. But I ended it when I came back!"

Sadhika! I knew her. She was his colleague. I have invited her over for dinner with her husband quite a few times. Our children have played together. The same Sadhika had a fling with my husband? Holy fucking shit!

"I guess this makes us even, right?" he asked hopefully.

Umm, it so did not. Because when he had that 'fling' I was fighting for our marriage. Doing anything and everything to keep his interest in me. But when I slept with Shlok, it was when Dhruv had outright betrayed me and practically announced that our marriage was over!

But this was not the time to harp about these things. Because I had one more confession to make.

"This is not it!" I whispered.

"You slept with more men?" he asked with raised eyebrows. "We can brush it aside and move on, for our kids' sake, Nyra."

Oh, my God! For our kids' sake... or for the reason that he literally, like at all, did not love me? Was he so unattached to me that he did not care that I've slept with multiple men? He did not care that other men touched my naked body? Rolled around with me in bed? Holy fucking shit!

But I just shook my head because I did not want to agitate him. He had cheated on me… he slept with someone, but I cheated on him too. Hell, I did something worse. And I have to tell him. I have to because no matter what, he was Dhruv! He was my husband. He was my best friend since the past sixteen years. And in no way I could go on without telling him what I truly did! Even if he was the one who betrayed me first… I have to tell him.

"Firstly, are you still having an affair with Sadhika?" I asked.

"Not really," he shrugged.

"We are platonic, you can continue with your affair, Dhruv, because what I did may force you to have one!" I sighed.

"What did you do, Nyra?" he asked with narrowed eyes.

"Promise me on our children's life that you will not repeat it to anyone, like ever," I insisted.

He nodded.

I took a deep breath and exhaled loudly. As I pulled at my hair very hard, I muttered the words I have been keeping to myself for days now, "I killed someone."

And as we went to bed, on our respective sides, Dhruv just stared at me. I had told him everything, starting from Shlok's father, to the poison, to the antidote and to the threat on our children. "So, you see, I had no choice but to kill him." I had begged for him to see reason and he had just nodded. There was so much going through my head as I stared at his face, which was partially in shadows now. And as I waited with bated breaths to see what he was feeling, he lay flat on his back and spoke, "Don't worry, Nyra. I know you did what you had to do. Because whatever you maybe, I know you are, first and foremost, a mother. You loved Shlok, so you are a lover. But I always knew you were something else too, and I have seen a hint of a psychopath in you quite a few times, but I am sure now, you are one. But given your good heart, you won't harm someone intentionally. So, it's okay. For all that you did. And believe me when I say this, I would never tell this to anyone, because, well, you are that *something else* after all." And chuckling lightly, he turned off the light, muttered goodnight and fell asleep. Like that!

35 AND THE LIFE GOES ON!

I returned to office and found it depressing. The mountain of work forced me to visit the office, but I was instantly haunted by the memories of better times. Tears filled my eyes, but I resisted. I had work to do and my life to get on with.

And as my eyes fell on Grisha, Roshesh, Vishal and all the others who were my mutual connection to Shlok, the memories of happenings of last week flashed in front of my eyes.

One week ago!

Knock! Knock! Knock!

The knock brought me back to this world. Shlok was lying next to me, wrapped under the same sheet as I was using to cover myself. I had not slept even for a moment last night and I was still reeling within. The way he had kissed me back the very first time our lips had met, I had felt the passion, the burning desire in him. The same that had been burning within me; the one I was not even aware of. The moment our lips had met, I had felt this was where I belong. He had paused before he pushed his hands inside my clothes; he had asked for permission. And it made me feel special. Despite me initiating it, he did not force me, he was truly the gentleman.

He did not push me to do anything, he did not force me for anything. But with him, I felt everything came naturally. It was not awkward at all. It was as if someone had unleashed a beast of desires within me and it was insatiable. And Shlok had given his all. With Shlok buried within me, I had found true pleasure, something I never even knew existed.

And there was a fierceness in him but he was still so gentle. And his touch was not rough, his touch was also not spark inducing as they showed in stupid movies, but it was so comforting that I felt a calm all over me.

And as I lay beside him now, after spending the whole night, the longest, happiest and most beautiful night of my life with him fighting over who would take charge time after time, I felt relieved and satisfied.

When he had taken me to bed, his eyes running up and down my body, I had felt conscious, I was fat now… quite bulky, to be honest. But he had no disgust in his eyes, instead all I saw was how he cherished me. How much he loved me. How much he desired me.

I have always fantasised about being held like this, loved like this—I wrote about this in my books—but it had never happened to me in the real life before. And though at the back of my mind, the guilt of cheating on my 'not-so-loving' husband was gurgling, I didn't let it push forward. I won't let my miserable reality burn my current happiness. Later I knew, I would feel the heat of it, but in the moment I was going to savour one last kiss from the man I so deeply loved, before he left and opened the door to whatever reality was waiting for us.

"Are you okay?" Shlok asked me sincerely as he raised his head and stared in my eyes. "I did not hurt you anywhere, right? I got carried away at times," he laughed sheepishly.

I pulled him and kissed him so deeply, so passionately that a moan mixed with an angry groan from the continued knocking at the door escaped his throat.

"Right now, I am perfect," I smiled on his lips, and he grinned back. "And I definitely want you get carried away like that over and over again."

Knock! Knock! Knock! and more frantic knocks.

"I wish I could have a forever with you," he whispered as he pushed his face in the crook of my neck, making me feel like I belonged in his arms.

"I think I lived my forever last night itself, whatever will come later will be a bonus," I smiled.

And he looked up and his eyes were so warm, so vulnerable, that I had no words to express.

But the increasingly getting frantic knocks forced him to pull away. He blinked and the look was gone.

"Coming," he groaned.

"I don't want to face whatever is out there, I want to live with you, in this moment," I whispered.

And his eyes, his beautiful brown eyes again had that warm, vulnerable look that I could not help it. I raked my hands on his bare chest, his perfect body, and he kissed me again.

But the person who was knocking would not budge or leave us alone.

So, cursing, finally he got up, wrapped a towel around his waist and opened the door.

And an incredibly angry Sheena barged inside.

"Get dressed quickly," she snapped as she rushed back outside, from where she shouted, "Here we are on the verge of life and death and you both are having sex, great!"

Shlok got dressed, and I did too. And when he opened the door for her again, he said, “Isn’t that the best time to have sex? It is like now or never, isn’t it?”

“Oh, shut it,” Sheena snapped. “He found you, didn’t he?” she asked me. And I nodded.

“So, what are you doing?” Sheena asked me again.

“I am going to kill myself,” Shlok suggested.

“NO!” both Sheena and I screamed.

“I will go to him,” I sniffled.

“NO!” this time Shlok shouted. “I would rip that man limb to limb if he touched you.”

“What other option do we have?” Sheena moaned.

“We could kill him,” a third voice came from the door. And a miniature Dhirendra Singh Rana stood there.

“Dinesh,” Shlok spoke suspiciously.

“Yes, big brother from another mother, me,” Dinesh grinned.

“Are you my sister-in-law now?” Dinesh asked me, and I stared at Shlok, confused.

“No, she is already married,” Sheena spoke scathingly.

“Oh, I thought the next time dad pulled this stunt, it would be with someone you truly loved,” Dinesh looked confused.

“I do love her,” Shlok spoke genuinely. “Hence, she is not going to him. Period!” he spoke the last words to his sister.

“In love with a married woman, sweeetttt,” Dinesh grinned, and Shlok gave him a ‘shut the fuck up look’!

“Fine,” Dinesh grunted, “she doesn’t want you dead,” he pointed at me, “and you won’t let her go to Rana!” he pointed at Shlok, who nodded.

“So, what do we do?” Dinesh clapped his hands dramatically and I found him weird! It seemed he was doing a part in a very expressive drama comedy!

“I have a plan, but for that, she indeed would have to go to him, and play her part,” Dinesh grinned deviously. “I have been planning this for a while now, so I have everything thought of, to the last detail. Are you in?" he asked me and Shlok.

"I am already in," Sheena shrugged.

"What is the plan?" I asked seriously.

"Umm, simple, kill that motherfucker!" Dinesh announced and Shlok just stared at him.

"You want to kill dad?" Shlok demanded. "Your own dad!"

"Umm, he is not my dad, well, biologically speaking he is, but he killed my real dad, you know, my mom's husband, the man who practically raised me till I was ten, then he snatched me from my mom. And then, he killed my mom when she refused to give me up. I mean I love *badi ma....*" He paused and added, "*Badi ma* is your boyfriend's birth mother, got it?" he asked me, and I nodded. "So, I love *badi ma*, but you do not forget when someone kills your own mother."

"Even though you inherit hundreds of billions in process?" Shlok asked with raised eyebrows.

"I would ask you the same question when someone would come after your mom, okay. Then you can tell me what it feels like to lose your mother," he spoke with a sting in his voice.

"He came to me earlier, I did not go to him," Sheena started. "He found out that dad was here, and you were here, so he put two and two together. He came to me with a plan, so I believe him," Sheena shrugged as she pulled out a nail filer from her bag and started filing her nails.

I mean, she was just standing there, filing her already perfect nails, while her brothers were talking about killing her father! Fuck!

Shlok looked at me, and then asked, "Are you in? I mean, you would be an accomplice in murder, but..."

"But that would save you a lot of emotional, mental, physical, psychological and not to mention sexual torture,"

Dinesh grinned. He looked like he was joking and having merry fun all the time.

"Would his death ensure no one else will come after you or my family?" I asked Shlok.

Dinesh just bobbed his head. "There are a few men who are loyal to him, but they won't know a thing. With Rana gone, they will fall in line, I know it. I have been pulling them on my side for years now," he informed.

"But?" I was confused.

"No one even knows he is here. Also, around the tent, no one would be there," he added.

"How do you know about the tent?" I asked suddenly.

"Because Rana always takes girls to a no-man's land. And he has already booked a private tent for a very secluded beach…." Dinesh snorted.

I blinked in shock. "He is right," Shlok nodded, "about the no-man's land," he added.

And I remembered that Rana had done this to three of Shlok's ex-girlfriends. And he had killed two of Sheena's boyfriends.

"The whole area will be roped off tonight," Dinesh continued. That pervert is paranoid, especially when fucking, I mean sleeping with girls half his age. Wants no proof. No one would know a thing!" he assured.

"How did he even know about me?" I asked.

"He knows because he had people stalking the siblings. He received photos of you with *bhai*. I was with him when he received them. His eyes all got gooey when he saw you. You look a lot like his fantasy type of girls," Dinesh pointed at me, and I shivered at the thought, "just add blonde hair and he would die at your feet."

"I am his fantasy?" I could not believe it. "ME?"

"Hey, who peed on your self-confidence?" Dinesh asked with a chortle. "Did you not instil some confidence in her when you instilled something else in her last night?" Dinesh gave Shlok a sly grin, to which Shlok shook his head in disgust.

"Shut up, Dinesh," Shlok barked, then took my hand and led me outside.

Once we were way far from their hearing range, Shlok started, "This would be dangerous, Nyra, very dangerous."

"I know, but it would ensure we all are safe, isn't it?" I whispered.

"Yes, but think this through, please. You would have to go to him, he would... he would..." and he trailed off.

"I don't think we have time to think about it," I sighed, trying to ignore and not think of what Rana would or could do to me within minutes of meeting him.

And as Shlok gave me a long, thoughtful look, I just held his hand and squeezed it.

"I would do anything to protect you and my family, believe me..." I started.

"And I would not let him touch you," he added.

I smiled. "I don't want him to touch me either," I whispered so softly that he just bent down and kissed me lightly.

"No, only I get to touch you now," he smiled. "And I really need to instil a lot of confidence in you," he grinned now.

"I cannot believe I am anything like a fantasy, even if of a pervert," I growled.

"You know you are very beautiful," he spoke with narrowed eyes.

"Hah!" I snorted, "I am fat, I am ugly, I am—" but he just placed his finger on my lips and said, "No. I fell for you when I first saw you. You are incredibly beautiful, kind, smart and courageous. You are also arrogant, defiant and a rebel, which just makes you even sexier. And this fat," he touched the flab of my tummy which always embarrassed me, especially last night, "this shows how brave you truly are. You have battled a life-threatening illness, and you have conquered two difficult pregnancies. Don't you dare belittle your body by thinking you are ugly or whatever. You are braver than most, and you should be proud of it."

"Oh, I could think of doing so many bad things to you right this moment," I whispered as I stared in his eyes, and he laughed.

"Hold that thought until we are done with this shit, alright," he laughed again.

"Should we go in, before they come out?" I asked seriously. With 'they' I meant Sheena and Dinesh.

"Are you really in?" he asked as he led me back inside.

"I am in…." I nodded at Shlok.

"Brilliant," and Dinesh clapped his hands as if he had already won. "So, what did Rana exactly ask you to do?" Dinesh asked seriously.

"He asked her to shave herself fully," Shlok spoke in disgust.

"Perfect, then shave. Even we do not want a loose strand of your hair sticking to his body or that tent later tying you to the scene, so, shave off," and he pulled out a couple of manual razors and an electric razor from his bag and pushed me to the bathroom. "Clean it off fully, even your head."

"What?" I asked, alarmed. "Can't I just wrap my hair in plastic or anything?"

"Umm, you cannot go to him with plastic tied to your hair. He is not stupid, you know. Also, hair falls all the time. What if any bit of hair gets stuck on his clothes?" Dinesh asked seriously. "Please, your perfect hair can grow back and believe me, my brother is not going to love you less if you are bald for a few weeks," he chortled. But when I just stared horrified, he added, "Fine, don't shave. But do tell what would you do with your long beautiful hair if you are locked behind bars. *Bhai* won't be there to rake his fingers through them, now would he?" Dinesh mocked.

I looked at Shlok, who looked uncomfortable, but nodded.

Resigned, I walked away wondering why Dinesh even had so many razors in his bag. It took me more than an hour to literally shave off every single hair on my body.

When I came out, feeling naked, even though I was fully dressed and had a scarf on my head, Dinesh asked me to take a long cold and hot shower, and change into something fresh. I obeyed.

He then handed me a black and a blonde wig. "Wear blonde before you meet Rana. If he asks, tell him you didn't wish to be identified on your way there. He would buy it!" Dinesh shrugged.

I nodded as I put on the black wig, it itched horribly but I endured.

"Now all you need to do is go to him, seduce him, and maybe flash your naked body to him to gain some control over the situation…" Dinesh explained.

Shlok tried to interrupt but I just shook my head. Of course, I would have to do it, why else would I have to shave myself so intimately! Also, I suspected he may even touch me, grope me, but I just prayed that Shlok and Dinesh would come in before things could progress much ahead.

That night, Dinesh first took Shlok and me to a different hotel. There we changed. He gave me an elegant wraparound dress to wear. It was so sleek and slender that the bulge of my stomach was visible from it. But I didn't bother. Last thing I wanted to do was look sexy tonight.

Dinesh, Shlok and Sheena dropped me outside the roped off space. Shlok did not let go of my hand that easily and I could sense how scared he was. Hell, I was scared too, but I just pressed my lips on his cheek and Dinesh pulled him back.

"Stay safe," he spoke sadly.

I nodded and walked ahead. The whole beach was secluded and dark, Dinesh did not lie about Rana's paranoia! The tent was pitched quite far from where the area was roped off, and I could see lantern kind of lights flickering inside the tent.

Harbouring tears of fear and disgust, I stumbled towards the tent. I was wearing nothing underneath the dress, so when I fell at one point in the dark, the sand from the beach actually slipped inside my holes! I cursed as I brushed off the sand as much as possible and stood at the mouth of the tent.

"So, you could not kill my son," Rana spoke in a lecherous tone. He was wearing nothing but loose shorts and was showing his round belly with pride. "I do not know what I want more, to fuck you or my son dead," he laughed. "Come inside," he added with a vile gesture.

I gulped and entered.

"What have you done to your hair?" he demanded as his eyes darkened, and I saw his bottoms twitch. He was getting an erection, the thought itself made me want to puke! But I persisted.

"So that no one recognises me," I spoke simply.

"Brilliant girl," he laughed as he gestured me to come closer to him. He was a head shorter than me, and his face reached my chest, which made it even worse!

He did not even ask, he just undid the strap of my wraparound dress and it fell open, dangling from my shoulders. He gasped as he raked my body with his dirty eyes. He grabbed my left boob and massaged it. It hurt, but I did not make a sound. He made to pull another one in his mouth, but I instead pressed my thumb in it.

He laughed as he bit on my thumb and started to suck it as his hand moved down in between my legs. But before his hands could reach there, his eyes seemed to fade and he fell on the ground with a loud thump.

I tied my dress back around my body and poking my head out of the tent entrance, I gestured randomly. Soon, Shlok, Dinesh and Sheena appeared.

Sheena dimmed the lights to the minimum so that the shadows won't reveal the happenings inside the tent. And then, Dinesh turned to me.

"May I?" he asked as he took a pair of tweezers and started to remove a thin plastic wrap from around my thumb. He had laced the plastic with a very powerful sedative. One that was his own creation, so assured to be practically untraceable in human body.

"Didn't I tell you that the sedative was very powerful," Dinesh smirked proudly. "All my studies as a chemist and running Rana's chemical business has finally paid off."

Sheena opened a plastic bag and Dinesh threw the tweezers and the plastic tape in it.

"I was scared you may accidentally chew on your thumb in nervousness. Good thing you did not," Dinesh chuckled.

"Wow! So much faith," I hissed.

"What?" he shrugged, "I have been observing you, you are a nervous nail biter," and he was right, I was chewing nails of my other hand now.

"Enough!" Shlok growled. And Dinesh bent down and pierced Rana's arm with a needle that was open at the other end. And from the other end, he pumped syringe after syringe of golden liquid. I could see his veins bulging as Dinesh was not patient and was literally plunging liquid in Rana's body mercilessly.

They had not made me privy of this part of the plan. Dinesh said it would be better if I knew the least, considering I was going to be in close contact with the bastard. And I was not too enthusiastic as well. I did not wish to know the finer details of this murder. And even now, as I saw them inject at least the twentieth dose of golden liquid in Rana's body, and it was not a normal syringe but a giant one, I still did not wish to know.

But my curiosity got the best of me because I asked, "Won't police know we have injected him with so much of something? I mean, that needle and so much liquid is going to leave marks."

Dinesh gave me an impressed look, then added, "Do you know what this liquid is?" he asked as he lifted the syringe for me to observe.

"Looks like alcohol," I commented. It smelled as such at least!

"Yes, but it is also laced with pure injectable heroin," Dinesh grinned. "I hope you know what heroin is?" he asked with raised eyebrows.

"Of course, I know! It is a recreational drug," I huffed.

"Good," Dinesh nodded. And somehow, even now, when we were in middle of committing murder, I wanted to smack his smugness!

"Enough?" Sheena asked, interrupting our conversation.

"Well?" Dinesh spoke and then he pulled out another bottle and pushed it down Rana's throat.

"But why?" I asked, alarmed.

"So even if they do find his body, it would look accidental. The injectable heroin in his body would explain the needle mark. It would look like he had overdosed way, way too much on alcohol and heroin, and had drowned accidentally," Dinesh grinned.

"But could he swallow what you tried to make him drink? It looked to me that most of that bottle's contents spilled out of his mouth," I wondered as I scrunched my face in disgust.

"This," Dinesh pointed at Rana's face, "is to lace his mouth and throat with it. Though what will come next will erase all traces of it for sure..." and he tried to hoist Rana's body, but to no avail. Sheena dimmed the whole lantern, and thankfully only a sliver of moon was visible in the sky, that too was getting covered with clouds every now and then, rendering the beach pitch dark.

The four of us dragged Rana's unconscious form to the water—his body was now reeking heavily of alcohol, so much so that it made me nauseous, or maybe it was because of the thought of what was going to happen next. As we got dangerously close to the deeper side, my heart started to beat even harder, but I swallowed. He threatened to kill my children, my family! He wanted to do vile things to me, and the memory of his hand on my breast brought more energy in my body.

"Bring out the chair, Sheena," Dinesh ordered. Everyone was wearing gloves, everyone except me. And as per Dinesh's explicit instructions, I had not touched anything in the tent, nothing at all as I did not wish to leave any fingerprints or any traces of DNA there.

Sheena brought out the chair from the tent. Her hair was tied and covered in plastic wrap too. I checked them all, they all were wrapped in plastic. All except for me, the thought crossed my mind again, making me more vulnerable.

"Clean his fingernails," Dinesh ordered.

"What?" Sheena shrieked.

"He touched Nyra," Dinesh barked, "which hand did he use to touch you, right, left or both?" he asked me.

I saw Shlok's eyes flip towards me in anger, but I ignored his gaze. I held my head high and spoke, "both."

"Clean both hands' fingernails, Sheena," Dinesh continued.

"But why?" Sheena exclaimed.

"DNA, sister, use that filer of yours and clean his fingernails," Dinesh ordered as he placed Rana in water and pressed his foot on his body. I saw in horror as Rana's entire body was now engulfed in water.

Sheena walked up to Rana's now slightly writhing body, and started plucking out from underneath his fingernails, gagging all the way.

"Done?" Dinesh asked.

Sheena nodded.

"Don't puke here," Dinesh ordered. "I don't think we can sanitise the shore in one night," he hissed.

And I could swear that Sheena swallowed the bile, I know I did.

"*Bhai,*" Dinesh spoke to Shlok, "clear the track marks," he ordered.

And I looked back, indeed deep gouge marks were there on the shore showing how four people have dragged something or someone very heavy to the water.

"How do you plan to go back?" I asked, shocked.

But Dinesh just stared at me as if I was asking an incredibly dumb question. He turned to Shlok and spoke a little loudly to make him hear, "Leave one set of footprints coming to the chair, and make them deep and staggered, considering his bulge and intoxicated state."

Shlok did the needful, and all the while, Rana stayed under water.

When all was done, Dinesh took out a stethoscope from his bag, and placing it in his ears he listened to Rana's heart.

"Dead," he diagnosed. "Shame, he died such quiet death."

And he let Rana's body go, which was now already filled with some water. And slowly, very slowly, we saw it get dragged farther in the ocean.

"We go away that way, sister," Dinesh spoke to me as he pointed to the very far side of the beach.

"What do you mean?" I asked.

"We will walk in the water for at least an hour, alright?" he spoke as he made me start to walk. "And then we would come out of water so that we do not leave our footprints or any trace to be tied back to that place. Understood?"

And we walked. But as I was wearing nothing but a sleek wraparound dress, I was practically shivering. So, Dinesh pulled out some clothes for me and I put them with help of Shlok. My body was numb with cold and what had just happened.

"Are you okay?" Shlok asked softly as he wrapped his hands around me for comfort.

"Your bother is a proper psychopath," I whispered.

"A psychopath who saved all your lives, you are welcome by the way," and Dinesh grinned so broadly that I sincerely prayed that this was the last time I ever met this guy.

We all went to our respective ways that night. I swapped my wig from blonde colour to black. Dinesh had found me another black wig, which was just like my original hair. He was a bloody mastermind, thought about every damn thing!

He had said to me earlier that day, "A perfect crime needs meticulous planning. And I have been planning it since the day he murdered my mother. So, believe me, there won't be a shred of proof that would tie us to his death."

And I sincerely hoped it did not.

And as we went to bed that night, I did not seek comfort from Shlok because I knew he too was still reeling with what we had done. But I did turn to him to ask if he regretted it? He just said no. He said, he regretted not doing it earlier and letting Rana ruin other lives. Shlok did not ask what Rana did to me when he touched me, and I was glad of it. While it could have been worse, the thought of his hand on my breast and another reaching down between my legs was imprinted in my mind. "Life goes on, Nyra," Shlok muttered. "Sometimes for the better, sometimes for the best, and this is for the best." And I knew he was right. And as I closed my eyes for the night, I knew for sure that my family was now safe, and that Rana would not torment any other girl ever in his life. No other girl will fall victim to that vile man. And in my mind, it was a big win.

EPILOGUE! WHAT WILL COME WILL COME!

I jumped out of the bed and wrapped my arms around Shlok's neck the moment he disconnected the call. He had brought me home from the office because I was getting upset by the moment. And now we were in his bedroom, where he was taking a call at his desk, while I was sitting on his bed, working.

"I am leaving in an hour," I crooned in his ears, and his head snapped in my direction.

"You are leaving already?" he asked seriously, disconnecting the call.

"It is already past six," I told him, and he turned around and pulled me in his lap.

"Hmm," he sighed, "I don't think I can ever get enough of you," he soothed.

He looked down and his eyes darkened. I was wearing nothing but rather short shorts and my black slip—the two pieces I had been wearing underneath my dress, which I had discarded the moment I had stepped in his house.

"Make the best of it then," and while his laptop started ringing again—which he just put the panel down—I pressed my lips firmly to his. He lifted me in his arms, I wrapped my legs around his hips, and he dropped me on his bed, climbing on top, kissing me hungrily.

"I love you," I moaned as he pressed one kiss after another on my already swollen lips.

"Not– more– than– I– do…" he groaned as he kissed me again, and again, and again.

"Are you okay?" Shlok asked as he drove me home. He insisted on dropping me home, saying it gave him more time with me. Which I appreciated more than he could even fathom.

I nodded. Things were back to normal with us. Today was the first day I had come back to office after that incident, and seeing people in office had overwhelmed me.

After that day at the tent, we had come back after an additional week. Dinesh had insisted that we stayed back in Goa, pretend nothing had happened and that we were just on a vacation. He believed that if we left that very night, police would mark us as number one suspect. But they could not. Because apparently Dinesh had planted alibis too. Before coming to the beach, Shlok and I had gone to a raging club, where we had entered through the front door, but had left after partying around a bit through a secret back door. Dinesh knew the owner, obviously! And after all that happened on that beach, Shlok and I had stepped back in the club through the back door, soaked ourselves in the alcohol, and well, had danced for hours. And all the while we danced, Dinesh and Sheena drove away from Goa, as if they were never here!

Police did not bother us much. But the news of Rana's disappearance did hit the media along with the news that his stepson was in Goa at the time, with his girlfriend. Thankfully, the identity of the girlfriend was kept a secret. But my tanned skin said a lot more than the media itself. But no one commented. People in office knew that Shlok lost his father, and he required condolences. As for his mother, his poor mother lost her husband again and was besides herself with grief. But none of her children told her the truth. They wanted her to live and die with a loving memory of her pathetic husband.

"You never told me what Roshesh said to you," Shlok asked me seriously. It was the fifth time he had asked me this today.

I just shook my head again, so he reminded me that we had decided on a trade-off. But when I still did not budge, he started to get angry. He was beside himself with rage when I blurted, "He was tricking me into signing a confession that you attempted to rape me in the medical room when we stayed in the office during the night of rains."

"What?" Shlok looked thunderstruck.

"Yes, he folded the paper carefully so I could not read it, but I snatched it from him. You did not promote him, so he wanted revenge," I sighed. "Pathetic, seriously."

And a mad glint appeared in Shlok's eye, one of which Dinesh would be very proud.

"He wanted to accuse me of raping you?" Shlok asked seriously.

"Dogs bark, Shlok, no use wasting time or energy over them," I tried to reason.

"Well, we took care of one problem, didn't we?" Shlok grinned, "I think in comparison to that, he is nothing… I think we can deal with it."

"NO!" I almost screamed, making the people on the road stare at us like we were crazy!

But Shlok just laughed. "Just kidding, love," he grabbed my hand, kissed it and winked. I felt an unease this time. I could feel waves of anger and hatred rolling off Shlok and it worried me.

"You would not do a thing, you know, to Roshesh, right?" I asked.

He raised his eyebrows, the way I always loved, and smirked. But he did not reply. He just drove past my society gates, and stopped the car to drop me off.

"Shlok?" I asked.

"Nah, I won't," he just shrugged. "I think he is not worth my time!" But somehow, I did not believe him.

"See you day after?" I asked seriously, digressing. I really did not wish him to hurt Roshesh. Pervert, bastard Roshesh maybe, but I really did not wish to add another murder to my kitty.

"You would stay the night, right?" he asked.

"Most probably, I will let you know," I smiled.

He squeezed my hand tightly, and then I hopped off the car.

As he drove off, I just stared after him. I had spent an incredible day in his arms, and yet I was so unsatiated. Damn, we lived so far from each other.... But I guess, it was for the best. I did not want my kids to know that they had a 'surrogate daddy' along with their own. I chuckled at the thought and walked home because no matter where my heart lay, I would always come back home, and my home was where my beautiful and precious children were.

And that night as we went to bed—me and Dhruv along with my children in our bed—I somehow knew Shlok was not joking when he said, 'we took care of one problem, in comparison to that, Roshesh is nothing'. I always knew I was a sociopath, I knew it now more because murdering Rana did not affect me as much as it should have. I did not get nightmares, I did not even get sleepless nights over it. Instead, once the shock had worn off, I felt a savage pleasure in murdering him, even if indirectly. And I knew I could do it all over again if people I love, especially my children, were ever threatened. But with the glint that appeared in Shlok's eyes, I felt that the sociopath in him had awoken too. A sociopath that Rana himself had created. But I did not bother about it. As of now, I had everything I needed in my life. My best friend, in form of my husband, who I was sure was rekindling a relationship with his ex. My beautiful children, for whom I would do anything and everything. And love in form of my boyfriend, Shlok. And while I do not know what turns my life would take, tonight, I do not think I could ask for anything more… because what would come would come, and this mother, lover and something else would face it head on….

THE END.

ACKNOWLEDGEMENT

First and foremost, I thank all the beautiful readers. It is because of your love and motivation that I have experimented with this story and have managed to write it in mere 8 days… I hope you find it as good as my other works.

My special thanks to my beloved husband, **Rajat Sharma**, for your love and evergreen support.

Big thanks and shout out to my beautiful kids, **Vihaan** and **Vanya.** For allowing me time to write and fuel my passion. Hoping when you read the story, way ahead in your future, you would like it.

My lovely nephews, **Dwij** and **Aadit**, your cheery smile and sparkling eyes always light up my day.

To my entire **family** for supporting me, motivating me, and making me what I am today.

My thanks to my editor and friend, **Priyanka Lal**, for your suggestions in this novel. Thank you for editing the book and helping me make it what it is today.

My big and special thanks to **Anuj Kumar**, my publisher and a very good friend, for all your support and encouragement.

And last but not least, a big thanks to the almighty for guiding me, blessing me, and making me what I am today.

ABOUT KRITIKA SHARMA

Kritika Sharma is a proud mother of two beautiful children. She is also an author, blogger, reviewer and a dreamer. Besides her writing career, she is also a marketing professional with more than a decade of experience.

She loves to read, write, and cook Indian delicacies for her foodie husband. Her every waking second is dedicated to her family, and yet she finds time for her passion, i.e., her books. She has published 12+ books across genres – Romance, Thriller, Non-Fiction etc. She loves to connect with her readers and is always available at

Email: kritikawrites@gmail.com

AuthorKritikaSharma

AuthorKritika

AuthorKritika

www.kritikasharma.in

MORE BOOKS BY KRITIKA SHARMA

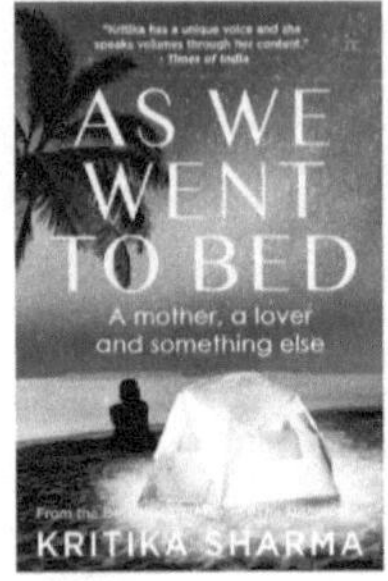

www.ingramcontent.com/pod-product-compliance
Lightning Source LLC
LaVergne TN
LVHW041021150826
845672LV00001B/166